James can't stand Wade. Wade is mouthy and pushy, and James would be happier if Chance had never allowed him to become a pack member. Unfortunately for him, Wade isn't going anywhere, which means James will have to learn to live with him.

That is, if he doesn't strangle him first.

Wade doesn't know why James hates him so much, but he tells himself he doesn't care. James is a stick in the mud, so why should he? It's better for him to focus on the promise he made to Dustin—finding Dustin's brother.

Since no one is willing to help Wade, he heads out on his own. He didn't count on James following him, and he certainly didn't count on falling in love with him.

Or on being kidnapped.

Stick in the Mud

ISBN: 978-1-4874-3960-6
Cover art by Angela Waters

Published by eXtasy Books Inc

Look for us online at:
www.eXtasybooks.com

Stick in the Mud
Mayport Pack 3

By

Catherine Lievens

Chapter One

"So who's moving into Dustin's room?" Matty asked.

Wade looked at him from his bed. He had to share his room with two of his friends, but he didn't mind. They were used to living together and in much worse conditions. It would be fine if he had to continue sharing his room with either Red or Matty.

Besides, Wade had every intention of moving out soon, too. He just needed to convince James they were made for each other and that he couldn't live without him.

Piece of cake.

"It doesn't matter to me," Red said. "Wade?"

"I'm fine here, so you decide. Or maybe we could give the room to one of the girls?"

"I already spoke to Josie, and they're fine rooming together. She's the one who said one of us should take it."

"Well, I don't care. I don't have a problem staying in this room."

Matty huffed. "You're not helping. I asked because I wanted an answer, but you haven't given me one."

"I did. I told you it doesn't matter."

"It doesn't matter to any of us, but someone has to make a decision. Why am I the one stuck doing that?"

Wade grinned at him. "Maybe you should be the one to move."

Matty looked tempted, which Wade understood. After everything they'd gone through, he wasn't surprised that Matty wanted some privacy. They might be used to sharing, but it didn't mean they loved it. Wade didn't mind, but Matty had always been more private and needed his time away from the others.

Wade and Red exchanged a glance. Wade was pretty sure Red felt the same about this, so he nodded.

"You take the room," Red said. "Wade and I are fine sharing, and we know how much you treasure your privacy."

Matty's cheeks flushed. "That doesn't mean I should be the one to take the room."

Wade got to his feet and stretched. "Just take it," he told Matty. "I'm pretty sure Red and I won't share for long, anyway."

Matty didn't look convinced. "You're still planning on seducing James?"

"Have you ever known me not to get what I want?"

"Not usually, but James is a tough nut to crack. He won't even talk to you, so how are you going to convince him to date you?"

"Little by little."

Thinking about James gave Wade something to focus on that wasn't feeling that he was losing his family. The conversation the three of them just had was about a room, but they'd been with the pack for a short amount of time. For now, most of their family still lived together, which was why they were discussing sleeping arrangements. Eventually, though, they'd drift apart as they found their place with the pack and started their new lives.

Wade had always expected that to happen. They'd been thrown together mainly because they'd all been homeless and alone. Banding together had given them strength, and it had kept them safe. Now, though, they didn't need to be safe. They didn't need each other anymore because they had the pack. They still stuck together because it was what they knew, but it wouldn't be for much longer.

Theo and Dustin were already pulling away. Wade didn't blame them, and in fact, he was happy for them. They all deserved love, but Dustin especially after what his family had done to him. Houston would be good for him, and they'd be happy together. It didn't matter that to do so, Dustin was leaving their ragtag family behind.

They were his past, while Houston was his future.

Wade started when a hand landed on his shoulder. Matty looked at him with a frown, and Wade forced himself to smile. "Don't worry about me," he said. "I'm fine sharing the room."

"This isn't about the room." Matty's tone was soft. "What's going on with you? You've always been stubborn, but you've latched onto James, and I don't get why. The guy is a dick, and he doesn't want us here. Why are you so bent on being part of his life?"

Wade's smile widened. It was more natural now, and he thought Matty could see that, because he relaxed.

"I'm sure there's a soft heart under all that assholery," he said. "And I intend to find it."

"Something tells me you'll have to dig *really* deep."

"That means I'll have fun." Wade winked. "You know me. I don't take anything too seriously, and the same goes for this. It's just fun to irritate him and watch his head explode."

"If you say so."

Matty didn't understand why Wade was having so much fun, and Wade didn't blame him. Sometimes, he didn't understand, either.

He wanted someone like Houston. He wanted to have someone who would love and cherish him, be there for him, and support him. He wanted someone by his side and to whom he could come back to at night. He wanted someone whose shoulder he could cry on but also someone to share his happy moments with.

He wanted what Dustin and Houston had, what Theo and Chance shared. He wanted to be loved, and that wasn't going to happen as long as he had his stupid crush on James.

So he had to find a way to get rid of that crush. Maybe if he and James gave in once, it would be enough to get him out of Wade's system.

Except that never worked in books. If anything, it led to more sex and everyone falling in love. It wasn't something Wade was against, so he'd decided to try anyway and see what happened.

A knock on the door distracted him. He could have kissed Dustin for the interruption, but Dustin wouldn't appreciate it. Instead, Wade beamed at him, which caused Dustin to blink.

"What did I miss?" Dustin asked.

"You're leaving and opening up a room. That means we don't have to share anymore, and frankly, I can't wait. Red snores."

"Hey!" Red complained.

"What? You do, and it's even cute, except when I have insomnia and it's three in the morning. That's when I'm tempted to strangle you, but I kind of like you, so I'd rather not."

Red rolled his eyes. "You *kind of* like me?"

"Have you heard anything from your brother?" Matty asked Dustin.

Wade had to resist the urge to snap at him. He'd been trying to stay away from the topic. Dustin already had a full plate, and he shouldn't be reminded of his missing brother.

He probably never stopped thinking about it. He was doing his best to go on with his life, but it was clear to everyone who knew him that he was worried. And who wouldn't be? His old clan had been attacked, and the dragons had been unable to shift. His brother had vanished, and their father had given up looking for him, if he'd even tried. The only one who cared about Dustin's brother was Dustin, and there was nothing he could do for him.

They didn't even know if he was alive. Wade found it strange that a powerful dragon shifter had vanished without leaving a trace, but he doubted anyone would listen to him. Besides, it wasn't like he had much to say. It was weird, but what could the pack do? If Dustin's father wasn't looking for his son, Wade doubted Chance would. He was a good alpha, but his priority was his pack, not Dustin's brother.

Dustin shook his head, his expression turning to sadness. "I've tried calling my father a few times to see if he had news, but he won't even answer. He told me he doesn't consider me his son anymore, and that was a relief until I realized it meant he wouldn't tell me anything about Mark."

Wade doubted Dustin's father had anything to say about Mark. His father didn't know who'd kidnapped Dustin's brother, and with the clan decimated, he didn't need an heir anymore. That was all he'd needed Mark for, and while Wade wasn't sure Dustin's father was happy to wash his hands of his sons, it felt that way.

But if he wasn't looking for Mark, who would? Wade had no doubt that eventually, Dustin would ask Chance to be allowed to go. Anything could happen to his brother in the meantime, though, and Wade didn't want Dustin to feel guilty about taking time, but the fact that the dragons hadn't been able to shift worried him. There had to be a reason for that, and it had nothing to do with the Mayport pack, no matter what Dustin's father believed. They were shifters, which meant they couldn't stop anyone from shifting.

Who could? That was the answer Wade had to find. The problem was that he didn't know where to start looking.

James scowled at the empty chair next to his. Houston should be there, but he was playing house with his new boyfriend instead. The thought annoyed James, but he wasn't surprised. His friend had always focused more on his personal life than on being the pack's beta.

"It's going to catch fire if you continue staring at it," Chance teased.

James forced himself to smile, but he doubted Chance would be fooled. "I don't know what you're talking about."

"Sure you don't." Chance leaned over his desk. "There's no way you're angry at Houston for finally being happy, right?"

James told himself that wasn't what he felt. He wasn't angry at Houston, and especially not for being happy with Dustin. Why would anyone feel that way? "I just thought he'd be here today," he admitted.

"He's moving Dustin in."

That would certainly explain why Houston wasn't anywhere to be seen. "Couldn't they do it over the weekend?"

"Why should they? Today is as good a day as any. Unless you have something against it?"

There was a note of warning in Chance's voice, which was why James was especially careful when he answered. "I don't have anything against Houston and Dustin being together or moving in together."

"Then what's the problem? You're always a sourpuss, but you've been getting worse over the past few weeks."

James was offended, but he didn't let it show. Even though Chance was his alpha and his friend, he didn't always understand him. James wasn't surprised. Like Houston, Chance led with his heart. He wouldn't have given Theo and his ragtag family a chance if he hadn't. He wouldn't have welcomed them into the pack, and he wouldn't have fallen in love with Theo.

James couldn't say things had worsened since Theo and the others had arrived, but he couldn't say they'd gotten better, either, at least not for him. Chance and Houston felt differently, but they got to go home to a man they loved every night. James only got to go home to an empty house, and it wasn't always fun, even though he liked things that way.

"I'm fine. We're all trying to find a new balance, and it's going to take a while." James made sure to smile at Chance, but they'd been friends for too long. There was no way Chance would be fooled.

Sure enough, Chance's lips curled into a smile. "You know you don't have to act as if everything is all right when it's not, right? You might be head of security for the pack, but you're still my friend, and that's even more important."

"Nothing is more important than keeping the pack safe."

"I don't disagree with you, but there's more to life than work. You just mentioned finding balance, but you don't have that in your life."

James crossed his arms over his chest and glared. This wasn't what the meeting was supposed to be about, and he didn't like the direction the conversation was taking. "I'm very balanced, thank you very much. Can we go back to talking about pack security now?"

But Chance was stubborn, and he ignored James. "You'll find someone eventually. I know there's no one in the pack you look at that way, but what about the newcomers? Theo's family are good people."

James's thoughts went straight to Wade, making him glare. Theo's family was nice enough, but Wade annoyed him like no one else did. He didn't want Chance to even think about pairing them together. The thought was enough to make him shudder.

"I'd rather focus on keeping the pack safe," he said.

"That's commendable, but it isn't the only thing you should have in your life. Eventually, you'll want and need more than your job, and I don't want you to be alone when that happens."

"You know me." James made sure his expression was softer. He didn't want Chance to think he was angry. "I'm fine on my own. In fact, I'd rather be on my own."

Chance looked skeptical. "I'm not convinced of that. I just think you aren't willing to give yourself the possibility of opening up to someone."

"Because I know it's no use."

For some reason, Chance smiled. "You'll see. One day you'll meet someone who will knock you off your feet, and you won't be able to stay away. You'll change your mind about being better off on your own then."

"I don't think so." James's job kept him in pack territory, and he'd grown up knowing every pack member. There was no one for him here, and considering how infrequently he left pack territory, he doubted he'd ever meet anyone. He was unwilling to consider Theo's family, so that was that.

He didn't need to meet anyone. He was fine on his own, and Chance needed to accept that.

James might have to do the same.

Sometimes, he *was* lonely and wished there was someone he could talk to, someone who would support him the way Chance and Theo supported each other. He couldn't afford to let anyone in, though. They would distract him, and that wasn't something he could accept. His main focus had to be his job and the pack.

"Who knows, maybe you've already met the person who will finally break down your walls," Chance teased.

"Please don't. I can't think of anything worse."

Chance laughed. "Eventually, you'll have to let someone in. Maybe Wade?"

"Don't ever say his name again. I don't want to think about him in any way, shape, or form."

"Why do you let him get under your skin like that? Just

mentioning him is enough to make you angry, and I don't get it. Unless you're trying to force yourself not to feel other emotions? Are you hiding all of them under anger because it's easier to deal with?"

James wasn't going to answer that. He wasn't even going to think about it. Instead, he straightened his back and looked down at his tablet. "With Houston distracted with Dustin, we need to go over the security measures again. He's going to be out of it for a few weeks, but I'm hoping that will be the extent of it. I'm ready to step into his position for as long as you need me to."

He carefully avoided looking at Chance because he didn't want to see his friend's disappointment. Chance was happy with Theo, and it made sense that he'd want both his best friends to be as happy as him. Houston was headed that way with Dustin, but there was no way James could do the same.

He truly was better off on his own.

Chance sighed. "Fine. We can talk about pack security and whatever else you have on your list. Don't think we're not going to talk about this again eventually, though."

"Talk about what? There's nothing to talk about."

"If you say so. I'm pretty sure there's *someone* to talk about, though. A young man with a big mouth and an even bigger heart. Maybe someone with curly blond hair and blue eyes?"

James gritted his teeth. "I don't want anything to do with Wade. He's annoying, mouthy, and a pain in the ass."

"He could be a pain in *your* ass."

James gaped. When had his friend become like this? Was it because of Theo? James liked Theo, but he wasn't sure he liked the changes in Chance as much.

His life had been easier before Theo and the others had arrived, and he still wasn't sure that welcoming them into the pack had been a good idea. However, there had been no changing Chance's mind, and James had stopped trying. Theo was here to stay, as was his family, and James needed to learn to live with that.

What he didn't need to learn to live with was Wade. The more space between them, the better it would be for James's sanity. As long as James focused on his job and ignored Wade, everything would be all right.

But why did it sound like James was trying to convince himself of that?

"I don't know what could stop someone from shifting," Dustin said.

They were having a last meal together. Houston and Dustin didn't live far, but it wouldn't be the same without Dustin living in the house.

Of course, it wasn't like Dustin had been spending a lot of time with everyone else. He'd always kept to himself, and that had only gotten worse since they'd become Mayport pack members. It was good to see him finally coming out of his shell, and they had Houston to thank for that.

Wade would make sure he did as soon as he saw Houston again. He didn't even care that Matty would move into Dustin's old room and free up space for Wade and Red. He'd known things would change when they arrived in Mayport, but it was still hard to wrap his mind around it.

But he would. This was his new life, and he needed to start accepting it. Dustin was moving out like Theo had, but they were both so close that they might as well still be living with them. If Wade wanted to talk to either of them, he just had to walk a few minutes, and he could. That was never going to change, just like the fact that they were a family wouldn't.

They'd been together through thick and thin, through living on the streets and trying to survive, and now, through becoming members of a pack. This was the best opportunity they could ever have found, and he couldn't begrudge Theo and Dustin for making the most of it. If he had the opportunity, he would, too.

But he doubted he would if James didn't get that stick out of his ass.

He decided he'd had enough of thinking about James, so instead, he focused on what Dustin was saying. He'd never heard of anyone being able to stop a shifter from shifting. Besides, who could do something like that? Not another shifter.

But maybe another magical creature.

He frowned, trying to think back to the stories his grandfather used to tell him and his sister. It had been a long time since he'd heard them, but he remembered they were about all kinds of supernatural creatures. Most had been shifters, but not all.

Wade remembered mermaids because they fascinated him when he was a child, but that wasn't what he needed. He doubted mermaids had anything to do with the dragons not being able to shift. That required being able to use magic, which could only mean one thing.

"Mages," he said out loud.

Everyone turned to him. Dustin had been about to bite his sandwich, and he blinked. Wade couldn't blame him for being confused. Most people believed that the stories about mages and other supernatural creatures were just stories. It would make sense for Dustin to believe the same, especially considering how much of a dickhead his father was.

"What are you talking about?" Red asked.

"Have you ever heard the stories when you were kids?"

"I wouldn't be asking if I had."

Wade glared at him. "Fine. I was just thinking about my grandfather and the stories he told Carrie and me. My favorites were about mermaids, but those aren't the only supernatural creatures he told me about."

"Mermaids don't exist," Matty pointed out.

"How do you know? I mean, we exist, and we're shifters. We have a kind of magic of our own, right?"

"I guess. That doesn't mean mermaids exist."

"Look, I don't know if mermaids are a thing, but mages have to be." Wade leaned forward, suddenly excited. "Think about it. How do shifters shift? How do we become our animal?"

"It's just something we do."

"Through *magic*. We can do something humans can't do, and the reason for that is magic. You have to know the stories about how shifters were first made, right?"

"I think we all do," Dustin said softly. "But they're just stories. I know some shifters believe it, but I never gave it much thought, and honestly, I don't want to. I just want my brother back."

"But think about it. If mages are behind this, they could have taken Mark. We just need to find out if there's a coven near your clan. If there is, you can be sure your brother is there." Because mages would do anything to hurt shifters, and a dragon shifter had a lot of magic. They needed to in order to be able to shift into such a massive animal. Wade was sure the mages could use that magic. He might not know how, but then, he was only a shifter.

He got to his feet, startling everyone around the table. "I need to see Chance," he declared.

"Why?" Matty was voicing what everyone seemed to think if their expression was an indication of anything.

They didn't believe Wade was right, but that was okay. Wade only needed the person in charge to believe him. That person was Chance, and as long as he gave him a moment to explain, Wade was sure the alpha would agree with him.

"I'll tell him about the mages. I'm sure he can send a few people to find the coven, and once we do, we can sneak in and get Mark back."

"Chance will never agree to that," Dustin pointed out. "He doesn't owe my brother anything."

"Maybe not, but he loves Theo, and Theo loves you. I'm pretty sure Chance would do anything for Theo, and there's also Houston to think about. He's one of Chance's best friends. Surely he wants Houston's boyfriend to be happy."

"I'm touched that you're taking this seriously, but I think you should leave Chance alone."

But Wade had made his decision. He needed to see Chance, and while he couldn't be sure where he'd find the alpha, he could start at the house where he and Theo lived. Chance had his office there, which was where he had most of his meetings and worked every day. If he wasn't there, Wade could start looking for him around pack territory, or even better, find Theo and ask him where his boyfriend was.

"Don't be rash," Matty tried to caution Wade, but Wade knew he'd figured it out. He just needed someone to agree with him.

He rushed out of the kitchen, already shedding his clothes. He almost dumped them on the bench by the door, but he realized he'd have to get dressed again to talk to Chance, so instead, he grabbed one of the bags from the bench and stuck his t-shirt into it. The strap of the bag was long enough to hang easily from his neck, and he quickly shifted once he'd finished putting all his clothes inside.

The world became just a tad smaller around him. In his okapi form, he was taller and saw everything differently. It wasn't better or worse, just odd, and like always, it took him a few seconds to wrap his mind around it.

As soon as he had, he ran in the direction of Theo's house.

It would have taken him about five minutes to get there in his human form. In his okapi form, he was there in just over two, and he was relieved to see Chance's car in the driveway.

That didn't mean he was home, but if he wasn't, Wade would just shift again and try to find him.

The front door opened before Wade could even shift back to his human form. Theo stood there, a brow arched, staring at Wade.

Someone had snitched.

Wade huffed and trotted up to Theo. He lowered his head and bumped it against his old alpha's forehead, relieved when Theo grinned.

Theo reached up to scratch the space between Wade's ears. "It's been a while since I saw your okapi form," he said softly. "But did you have to shift? Our houses aren't that far."

Wade rolled his eyes. Theo was a shifter, so he understood that sometime, shifting was necessary. Wade was hyped up by his idea, and he'd been excited about talking to Chance. Shifting and running in his okapi form had allowed him to release some of that energy, but now, it felt like it had come back, itching under his skin.

He shifted back to his human form and stuck his tongue out at Theo. "Who snitched?" he asked as he unhooked the bag from around his neck and dug out his clothes.

"Dustin. He said something about mages, but I have no idea what he was talking about."

"I can't believe you don't know the stories about the mages, either. Are you guys sure you're shifters?"

"I didn't know about them, but something tells me that's not going to last for much longer."

There was sarcasm in Theo's voice, but Wade ignored it. "You're right. I'll tell you everything there is to know about mages."

And hopefully, Theo and Chance would believe him. He needed them to for himself, but more importantly, for Dustin.

The office door slammed open, making James jump in his seat. His first instinct was to get to his feet and place himself between Chance and the door, even though he didn't know who had just barged into their meeting. He needed to protect his alpha, and he'd happily give his life to do just that.

But he didn't have to because Wade stormed in. His eyes were wide and his hair was all over the place, and the sight of him made James want to growl as much as it made him want to tug him into his arms.

James couldn't be weak. It didn't matter how adorable Wade was. He was also annoying, and he shouldn't be here.

James took a relaxed posture and put his hands on his hips. "Don't you know that polite people knock on the door before barging into a room?"

"Don't you know that normal people have fun?" Wade sniped back.

James stepped toward him, not even thinking about what he was doing. A hand on his shoulder made him stop, and when he turned to Chance, his friend tilted his chin toward the chair he'd been in earlier, silently telling him to sit again. James wasn't embarrassed by the fact that he'd put himself in front of Chance. This time, it had only been an annoying little shit, but it could have been an enemy.

James huffed and flopped into the chair, still glaring at Wade. Wade wasn't looking at him anymore, though. His focus was on Chance, and considering how agitated he was, James suspected nothing good would come out of whatever was happening.

"I think I know who took Dustin's brother," Wade announced.

James stared, not knowing what to think. How could Wade know? No one did—not even Dustin's father, and he was the alpha of his clan.

"Why don't you sit down?" Chance asked.

His gaze moved to the door, and James realized Theo hovered there, clearly unsure whether he should come in.

One wave from Chance and Theo was in. He didn't bother to close the door since they were the only people in the house, and he made a beeline for Chance, sitting on the arm of his chair. Chance wrapped an arm around Theo's waist, and James had to look away.

He didn't have time for a relationship, and he didn't want one, but he couldn't deny that sometimes, he was jealous of the easy affection between Chance and Theo.

"Start from the beginning," Chance said.

Wade beamed as if Chance had handed him the moon. "We were talking about it while Dustin was packing his things, then over lunch. Everyone's wondering who could have blocked the dragons from shifting, and only one explanation makes sense."

Wade paused and peered at Chance as if he expected him to say something. Chance appeared confused, though, and he wasn't the only one.

Wade huffed and shook his head. "Come on. You're older than me, so you have to have heard the stories."

"Why don't you tell us about them?" Chance asked.

Wade finally sat down. James wanted to tell him to leave because he and Chance still had work to do, but one glance from Chance was enough for him to press his lips together. He wasn't the alpha, and he wasn't the one who made the decisions. That was a good thing because he didn't think he would have been able to deal with the pressure, but sometimes he wondered what went through Chance's mind.

"My grandfather always told me the stories when I was a kid about how shifters were born. Everyone knows that the mages created us because they were lonely and wanted companions that would never leave them."

James *had* heard the stories, although he didn't remember

them well. Like Wade, his grandparents had told them to him when he was a child. It had been years since he'd thought about them, though, and he couldn't see what they had to do with Dustin's brother.

He wasn't the only one, because Chance looked just as lost as he did. Theo appeared confused, too, and after Wade waited for a moment, he huffed and crossed his arms over his chest. "You really don't know? Come on. The legend goes that mages created shifters with their magic, which means shifters *are* magic. It's what enables us to shift. Eventually, though, shifters had enough of being nothing more than pets, and they rebelled. There was a war, and many mages and shifters died. Shifters were able to thrive after that, while mages went into hiding. Everyone knows they want revenge and that they hate shifters. They were hunted, and that wasn't right, but what they did wasn't, either."

"I'm not sure what this has to do with Dustin's brother," Chance said delicately, as if he was trying not to hurt Wade's feelings.

There were reasons he was the alpha while James wasn't, and it wasn't just because his father had been the alpha before him. He was just a better person than James could ever be, and that was fine. James didn't need to be nice. He needed to be fierce and protect the pack.

He just wasn't sure what he was supposed to protect the pack from in this situation.

"Don't you see? It has to have been mages. Who else could stop the dragons from shifting? If it was one dragon or even two, it could have been a coincidence or whatever, but the entire clan? It's just not possible, which means it was magic. There's no other explanation."

James snorted. "Just because you say there isn't, doesn't mean that's the case. Do you really believe what you're saying?"

Wade's eyes narrowed. "I wouldn't be here if I didn't believe it. I don't see what else it could have been. Mages have magic and created shifters, so they would know better than anyone how to stop them from shifting. From there, it would have been easy for them to take over the clan and kidnap Mark. A dragon shifter has a lot more magic than someone who can shift into something smaller, so they might use him as a battery or something, or maybe they took him to torture him. Mages aren't good people."

James had to work hard not to laugh in Wade's face. There was no way anything he was saying was true, but it wasn't his place to point that out, so he turned to Chance.

Chance still looked confused but not opposed to what Wade was saying. James couldn't believe he was even thinking about this. It just wasn't possible, and Chance had to see that.

"This is ridiculous," James said.

"Just because you think you're right doesn't mean you are," Wade told him. "You're only one person, and not a nice one at that. You don't know everything that's in the world, and I'm sure that if there are mages out there, they wouldn't come to you and introduce themselves. If anything, they'd probably kidnap your ass to use you as a battery."

"They could try."

"You know, I don't think they would. They wouldn't want to deal with you, and I wouldn't blame them. No one in their right mind wants to deal with you because you're a dick."

"Now listen here, you little shit—"

"Enough." Chance's voice was strong. "James, if you don't have anything to add to the conversation, I suggest you go."

James gaped. "What do you mean? We were having a meeting."

"I'm aware of that, but it doesn't matter. We were almost done, and I want to listen to what Wade has to say."

"You have to see this is foolish. There's no way there's a band of mages hanging around kidnapping shifters. It doesn't make sense. Life isn't a storybook."

Chance sighed and pinched the bridge of his nose. "Please. I'll call you later so we can finish the meeting, but right now, I feel the need to separate you and Wade."

Wade looked smug, which made James want to throttle him. Instead, he clutched his tablet to his chest as he got to his feet. "I'll see you later," he said rigidly.

Chance rolled his eyes, but James didn't try to change his mind. He hadn't been talking as James's friend just now, which was why James was treating him as the alpha. If Chance wanted to listen to Wade's stories, then it was his prerogative to do so. Luckily, James wouldn't have to stick around and do the same.

He had better things to do.

Chapter Two

Wade usually looked forward to spending time with his family. Now that they'd moved in with the Mayport pack, he didn't see them as often as he used to, and he missed them. He was happy to see all of them tonight, but he was a bit wary after he met with Chance.

The alpha had listened to him. Wade had known he would, if anything, because of Theo. However, Chance hadn't been convinced about what Wade was saying, and Wade didn't know what to do. Should he insist that the reason the dragons hadn't been able to shift during the attack was magic? Should he let it go? He was convinced he was right, because nothing else made sense. There was no other explanation than mages, but it felt like no one believed him, and it made him angry. It was also disappointing, but he was used to being disappointed.

The problem was that he felt he could be useful. If the mages were involved, they could find Dustin's brother. He had to be somewhere out there, probably being hurt. Why did no one realize that? Why didn't they agree to help? Even if Wade was wrong and mages had nothing to do with what had happened to the dragons, Mark was still gone. Dustin seemed to be the only one who wanted to help his brother, but even he was busy with his new life.

Wade didn't blame him. After what he'd learned about Dustin's family, it made sense for Dustin to want some distance between them. Dustin was worried about his brother, but it felt like he'd already given up.

Wade hadn't.

But tonight wasn't the night to focus on mages and whether they were real. Wade had a family dinner with Theo, Chance, and everyone else, and he was counting on talking to Chance again. He hadn't been able to convince him the first time around, but maybe the second time would be more successful.

He wasn't asking Chance to send half of his pack over there to find the mages and Mark. He just wanted Chance to allow him to fully explain and, more importantly, to believe him.

"I don't like that expression," Red said as he gestured at Wade's face.

Wade scowled at him. "That's my face. I was born with it, and I can do little about it."

"You have that expression you always have when you're planning something. It's never a good thing, and I'm worried."

Wade looked at his reflection in the mirror one last time before turning to his friend. He put his hands on his hips and glared at Red, but Red didn't seem to care. He wasn't cowed at all, but Wade supposed he wasn't scary to someone he'd lived with for a while. Red knew Wade had a marshmallow heart and that he'd never hurt anyone. He also knew Wade was stubborn when he wanted something, and he wasn't wrong. Wade *was* plotting something.

He needed Chance to believe him.

Red sighed. He was wearing jeans and a dress shirt, which was odd to see on him. It was even odder to wear something similar, albeit in different colors. Before, everyone had worn whatever clothes they could find, and they seldom fit them. Wade remembered a dark blue sweater that had been three sizes too big for him, but he'd worn it until it had fallen apart.

He wasn't wearing an oversized sweater anymore. He had on jeans that clung to his legs and a shirt the same color as his blue eyes, and he looked good.

Sometimes he had trouble recognizing himself in the mirror. It was weird, because he knew that the person looking back at him was himself, but it didn't look like it. Hopefully, his brain would eventually learn to deal with it, because he wasn't looking forward to feeling like this for the rest of his life.

"What are you planning?" Red asked. He sounded resigned, which made Wade bristle.

"I'm not planning anything, I swear. I'm looking forward to a nice evening with the others and Chance."

"You're going to try to talk to him about the mages again, aren't you?"

"Why won't anyone believe me? Mages are real, and they have Dustin's brother. We need to help him."

Red raised his hands. "I never said I don't believe you. I'm cautious because I never thought mages were real, but I suppose anything is possible. They might even have Dustin's brother. But what can we do about it? Do you want to go out there and rescue him yourself?"

Wade was starting to think it was the only way to do this. He didn't tell Red that, though. He didn't want people to worry, although they would if he suddenly disappeared without telling anyone where he'd gone.

"I just want people not to look at me like I'm nuts," he groused. "James didn't even listen to me. He told me right off the bat that I was wrong, and that was that. Can you believe it?"

That seemed to amuse Red because he smiled. "You mean the same James who you've been bickering with since we arrived in Mayport? That doesn't sound like him at all."

Wade glared. "All right, so I'm not surprised he wouldn't listen to me. But why does he have to be so rude all the time?"

"I don't know, but if you're going to seduce him, you'll

have to find a way around that."

Wade wasn't sure he wanted to seduce James anymore. It had sounded fun in the beginning, but considering the way James was treating him, maybe it would be better for Wade to stay away.

"Guys? Are you ready to go?" Matty asked from the hallway.

Wade strode over to the door to open it. "Yeah, we are." It wouldn't do him any good to stay back and obsess over this. Whether Chance believed him or not, he'd have to do something, but he still didn't know what. He needed time to think about it.

Almost everyone was already gathered in the entrance of the house they shared. Wade went over to his sister and hugged her, but she was busy talking with Josie, so he left her to it. Once everyone was there, they headed out and followed the path that would lead them to Chance's house, which they reached not even five minutes later.

For the first time tonight, Wade wondered who else would be there. He wasn't surprised to see Dustin and Houston arriving from another path, and he waved at Dustin. Dustin waved back, looking more relaxed than Wade could remember him being. Houston was doing him a lot of good, and Wade couldn't find it in himself to be sad that Dustin had left them. He wasn't far away, and he was happier than he'd ever been, which was worth everything.

Seth had already knocked on Chance's door, and Theo opened it. He hugged everyone as they walked in, directing them toward the dining room. Wade was the last, and he quickly hugged his friend before stepping into the house.

Theo grabbed Wade's shoulder to stop him. Wade sucked in a breath, knowing he wasn't going to like this. He still plastered a smile on his lips.

"Wade, you know that I love you," Theo began.

Wade snorted. "What happened? Did someone die?"

That made Theo smile. "No, but someone might, since James is attending this dinner, too."

Wade groaned. He'd known it was a possibility, since James was one of Chance's best friends, but he'd done his best to ignore it. "I promise I won't start anything."

Theo's eyes narrowed. "That's not what I want from you. I want you to promise you won't fight with him at all, not even if *he* starts it."

"That's not fair. What am I supposed to do if he bothers me? Ignore him?"

"Yes. And please, don't antagonize him. That's always how it starts, and while I understand why you find it fun to annoy him, I don't want the two of you to fight tonight. This is a family dinner, and both of you are members of our family. I don't expect you to become best friends, but I'd like both of you to be at least civil with each other."

"He's an asshole with a stick up his ass," Wade muttered. He didn't think anything could change that. James was hot, but he was an asshole, and Wade seemed to be the only one ready to tell him that. He didn't understand how Chance and Houston had ever become friends with him, but then he hadn't grown up with them. Maybe he'd know if he had.

"Please," Theo begged.

Wade sighed. "Fine. I'll be nice."

"I suppose I can't ask for more."

Wade wanted to promise everything Theo wished for, but he couldn't. If James bothered him, he wouldn't hesitate to snap back.

The ball was in James's court.

James watched as everyone streamed in. He nodded at a few people but didn't get up from his chair to welcome them. It wasn't his place, since this wasn't his home, and besides, he wasn't close to Theo's family.

He kept his gaze on the door, waiting for Wade to make his entrance. He had no doubt the man would be here, so it was odd not to see him right away. James would have imagined Wade would be the first one in. He enjoyed being the protagonist of whatever was happening and was always incredibly noisy.

But there were no signs of Wade by the time everyone was in. For a moment, James wondered if maybe he'd stayed home. It would be too good to be true, so he had no faith in that. Wade probably thought everyone would pay attention to him if he walked in late. Well, James wasn't going to do that. He found it incredibly rude when people were late, and he wasn't surprised Wade was one of those people. He had no respect for anyone, something James had realized the first time he'd met him.

"No Wade tonight?" he asked Chance, who was mixing drinks next to him. "I'm surprised. I expected him to come and start talking about that mage thing again." He snorted and took a sip of his beer. "Can you believe it? He has to be nuts to think mages are real."

The room fell silent, and James looked around. He sucked in a breath when he saw that Wade had entered with Theo, and both of them were glaring at him. Theo's expression didn't stay that way for long, though. Seconds later, he was reaching for Wade, but Wade shook his hand off.

"No," he said. "I'm sorry, but he's the one who started it. I promised you I'd be nice and had every intention of doing just that until I walked in and heard him."

Wade looked angry, and for some reason, it gave James a certain satisfaction. He liked getting under Wade's skin, even though he didn't understand why.

"I don't get how Chance and Houston can stand you

because you're a dick," Wade continued. "Honestly, it's not a surprise that you don't have anyone in your life. Who would want to be with you?"

James was offended, even though he didn't want a relationship. It wasn't because he couldn't have one, though. It was because he didn't want one, but Wade probably didn't understand that.

"Enough," Chance snapped. "I don't want to hear either of you talk to the other tonight. This is a family dinner, and you're both part of our family, but I won't let you ruin it. If you can't be nice to each other, I'm going to have to ask you to leave."

Wade crossed his arms over his chest. "I can be nice. I was going to be until he started it."

"We're not children," James said. "*He started it* isn't a thing."

"Just stop it, please," Chance said. "I don't know why you hate each other so much, and honestly, I don't care. I just want to have a family dinner, and I'm going to kick you out if you're not nice."

Wade smiled at him. "I apologize. Have you thought about what I told you about mages?"

James pressed his lips together. He'd just promised he wouldn't needle Wade, and he had to keep that promise, even though it was hard.

How could Wade not see how ridiculous this was? Mages didn't exist, just like mermaids and fairies didn't. Only a child would believe in those, and Wade was in his mid-twenties, an adult who needed to contribute to pack life.

That reminded James that he wasn't sure Wade had a job yet. He'd have to ask Chance, because if Wade expected the pack to support him without him doing anything, James would be happy to point out that wouldn't happen. It didn't matter that Wade was part of Theo's family. If he couldn't contribute, then he had no place with the pack.

"Wade," Chance began.

"Look, I know it sounds too weird to be true. I haven't met a mage, and I only have my grandfather's stories to go by. That doesn't mean they don't exist or that they don't have Dustin's brother. If you could just send someone there to check, I'm sure you'll find out that I was right, and we'll be able to help him. That's what matters, isn't it?"

James couldn't help it. He snorted, but when Chance glared at him, he mimed locking his lips and throwing away the key. He wouldn't antagonize Wade, even though what Wade said was stupid. He'd promised, so he'd let Chance deal with that by himself. His friend had wanted Theo's family to move here, and unfortunately for him, that family included Wade. Chance had to deal with him like he had to deal with every other pack member.

Better him than James.

"I understand why you're worried, and the fact that you feel that way for someone you don't know is commendable, but I can't just send someone out there. You have to see that, Wade. My main focus is the pack and keeping this place safe." Chance sounded reasonable.

Wade was anything but, so James wasn't surprised when he insisted.

"But Dustin is one of your pack members. Why don't you want him to find his brother?"

"I do want him to find his brother. I don't trust the dragons, especially after they accused us of attacking them. Anyone I might send there would risk getting hurt, and that's not something I can allow to happen."

"Then maybe they don't have to go on their own. You could send someone else with them. I'd be happy to go and help however I can."

James could imagine how that would end. He didn't think

Chance wanted to risk that disaster, especially considering the kind of person Wade was. He was adorable, but clearly, that didn't make him smart.

"I'm sorry," Chance said. "I can think about it, but I don't believe I'll change my mind. We can't trust the dragons, and I won't put anyone in danger."

Wade opened his mouth, no doubt to argue again, but thankfully, one of his friends grabbed his arm and pulled him away. James watched them go, knowing this wasn't over by any means. Wade wasn't the kind of person who let go of something like this, but thankfully, it wasn't James's problem. Chance had made that clear, and James would be more than happy to stay away from Wade.

"You know, you don't have to look so smug," Houston said as he sat next to James.

"I'm not smug."

"Your expression begs to differ. What do you have against Wade, anyway? He's a nice kid. He's doing his best to help Dustin and has never been part of a pack like ours. He doesn't understand what it means or why Chance is saying no to his request. Instead of making fun of him, you could explain."

"Chance just did, and if he couldn't get through to Wade, I don't see how I would be any different. Why would Wade listen to me?"

"You're not wrong. You've been an ass to him since they got here, so why would he?"

"I wasn't an asshole. I just need to keep the pack safe."

"You don't have to do that by putting him down every time he says something."

"That's not what I'm doing, but someone has to keep his expectations down. He's not going to be able to be part of the pack if he doesn't understand his place here."

Houston arched a brow. "And what would that place be?"

James shrugged. "He's the one who has to find it. He needs

to start respecting his alpha, though, and that means not bothering him when he's been clear. Chance isn't sending anyone, and it's the right decision." Especially since Wade still believed in fairies and mermaids. Mages weren't a thing. Every shifter in the world would know about them if they were, but the only thing James had ever heard were stories, and everyone knew stories weren't real.

Everyone except Wade, apparently.

Wade wasn't angry at Chance. He understood the explanation Chance had given him for not wanting to send anyone, and he couldn't blame him for not wanting to put his people in danger. He was the alpha of this pack, and his main job was to keep the pack safe. Dustin's brother wasn't a pack member, which meant Chance wouldn't risk anyone to help him.

But Wade wasn't finished attempting to convince him. He gave Chance some space, allowed everyone to relax, and waited for the best moment. It came after dinner when everyone was still at the table. Wade was close to Chance, and he leaned over, his question ready.

"What if someone volunteered?"

Chance didn't ask what Wade was talking about. He obviously already knew. "How can I ask anyone to volunteer for something like this?"

"You wouldn't be forcing anyone. You'd be asking them if they were willing to do this, and I'm sure someone would be." If anything, Houston would probably want to go. He was in love with Dustin, so he knew how much pain Dustin was in at the thought of his brother being gone.

"Do you still not get it?" James asked from Chance's other side. "We won't be sending anyone. I'm sorry for Dustin, but his clan was decimated, and his brother is probably dead. Nothing we do can help with that."

"You don't know if he's dead. We don't know anything, because you refuse to send someone."

"Chance is making the right decision. He's choosing to protect the pack, which is what he needs to do. I'm head of pack security and agree with not sending anyone. It would be stupid to put someone in danger that way."

Wade snorted loudly. "How can I not know that you're head of pack security? You keep telling everyone as if it makes you more important. Well, you're not more important than me. You're not more important than anyone."

"I beg to differ. I'm head of pack security, and that's a vital job. If it wasn't for me, the pack wouldn't exist. Do you know how many times I've protected it from attackers?"

"No, and frankly, I don't want to hear it. You just want to sing your own praises, although that's probably because no one else will do it. Everyone hates you too much."

A few people around the table sucked in a breath, and Wade felt guilty. He'd promised he wouldn't bicker with James, but what was he supposed to do? Sit back and allow James to insult him? He was too angry to do that, and someone needed to give James a good smackdown. He was a dick, and that wasn't going to change if no one stood up to him.

"I have no doubt *you* hate me, but you're little more than a child. Everyone else is adult enough to know that I'm the best man for the job."

There was scorn in James's voice, and Wade had to resist the urge to grab his fork and stab him with it.

Maybe he didn't have to resist. James was a shifter, so surely, stabbing him a few times wouldn't hurt him. Besides, it would be with a fork. Wade could have gone for the knife he'd used to cut his meat, but even he wasn't that much of an asshole. He just wanted to wound James a little and make him bleed, not to hurt him too badly.

Although that might change if James didn't stop being an

asshole.

"I'm not a child," Wade snapped. "I'm twenty-five and have more life experience than you can ever dream of." He'd lived on the streets for years, and he'd survived. There was no way James would have been able to do the same.

James looked smug. "Like I said, a child. I'm thirty-nine, and I've been head of pack security for a decade. I'm also pretty sure that being more than a decade older than you means *I* have more life experience."

"You certainly have more experience at being an asshole. That's why everyone avoids you. You should hear what they say behind your back."

James didn't flinch, but a flicker of something in his expression told Wade he'd touched a raw nerve.

Good.

"Enough," Chance ordered.

Wade snapped his mouth shut. *Dammit.* He'd made a promise, and he hadn't kept it. Chance was pissed, and he had every reason to be. Wade was ashamed of his behavior, even though James was responsible for a lot of it. Why couldn't he leave Wade alone? Why did he always have to harass him until he made Wade snap?

"Wade, I'm sorry, but I'm not willing to risk my people and send someone out there to find the mages, even if they're real. We don't know what the dragons would do to them, or if the mages are real, what *they* would do. Someone attacked the clan, and they were powerful enough to block the dragons from shifting and kill most of them. Even if I decided to send volunteers, I would be putting them in danger, and it's not something I'm willing to do."

Chance truly sounded sorry, and that made Wade feel even more guilty. The alpha wasn't done, though.

"While I appreciate how much you care about this and how much you want to help Dustin, you and James need to stop. You're making everyone uncomfortable, and frankly, I don't think anyone would argue if I were to decide not to invite either of you to the next family dinner."

"I'm sorry," Wade whispered.

"You should be," James said, sounding like he'd won.

He couldn't have been more wrong, and Wade had to resist the urge to grin when Chance turned his attention to him.

"And you. Like you just said, you're an adult, or at least, you're supposed to be. Yet, every time you're with Wade, you become a child again, and I'm done dealing with that. I don't care what your problem with Wade is. You need to get over it before I decide to stick the two of you in a room and lock the door until you fix this. Honestly, you make me wonder if I've made a mistake by making you head of security. You're too childish to be responsible for such a vital job."

Wade had to bite the inside of his cheek not to grin at the look on James's face. It wouldn't help to start another fight, and he was pretty sure Chance *would* kick both of them out if he did.

Wade didn't have anything against James. He didn't know why James had been such an asshole to him since the first time they'd met, but he wasn't about to ask. Once, he'd thought maybe they could work things out together. He'd believed that James treated him that way because he didn't know him, and he'd thought that would change if he gave James a chance.

It hadn't. Every time they spoke, James put Wade down. He thought Wade was childish and an idiot, and he hadn't given him the opportunity to show he wasn't. Why he hadn't didn't matter. Wade was tired of trying to find the reason behind this hate. At this point, he just wanted James to fuck off and leave him alone, but even that was too much to ask for. Every time Wade opened his mouth and James was there to hear what he was saying, James had a snarky answer.

Maybe it would be good if Wade left the pack for a bit. He

wanted Mayport to be his home, so he wouldn't be gone forever, but since Chance was unwilling to put any of his people in danger to find Dustin's brother, Wade would have to take things into his own hands.

It sounded like a bad idea, but Wade's life was a collection of bad ideas. No matter what James thought of him, he could protect himself, and he would. Then when he'd come back with the proof that mages were real and maybe that they had Dustin's brother, everyone would have to believe him, including James.

Wade would show him that he wasn't an idiot. He'd show him that he needed to respect him, and James would have to.

James looked down at his hands. Chance was right. He was behaving like the child he'd accused Wade of being, and he was ashamed of himself.

He didn't know what it was about Wade that pushed him to behave like an idiot. Wade was the only person James ever behaved like this with, and he didn't understand. It was as if someone else took control of his mouth and spouted things that he knew Wade would find offensive. He also knew Wade would answer, and it was exhilarating to think that he could push someone to the brink of yelling at him like that.

But feeling that way made him an asshole. Not listening to his alpha was even worse, let alone the fact that he and Chance were friends.

"You know you can trust me to protect the pack," he told Chance.

Chance was still angry. "I'm starting to wonder. Everything was fine until Wade arrived, and please, don't tell me that everything will be fine if he leaves, because I'm not kicking him out. He's Theo's brother."

"They're not related," James pointed out.

If looks could kill, Chance would have *unalived* James right at that instant. "They might not be related by blood, but it doesn't mean they're not brothers, just like it doesn't mean that you, Houston, and I aren't brothers. What's going on with you? You've never behaved this way, and I'm failing to understand what's happening."

James shook his head. "I don't know. Nothing."

"Clearly, it's not nothing if you react like a child every time Wade opens his mouth. It's like you're pulling on his pigtails or something." Chance's eyes widened. "Is that what's happening? Because let me tell you, it's a dickhead thing to do. Boys don't pull on girls' hair because they like them. They do it because they're assholes, and if that's what's happening, I have to tell you that it's not going to endear you to Wade."

"I *don't* like Wade," James snapped, loud enough that half the table heard him. He didn't care. He needed everyone to know that he didn't like Wade. "He's a child, and there's nothing attractive about him."

"I feel you're protesting a bit too much for that to be true, but fine. I'll let it go. You need to stop this, though, whatever reason you have. Wade is a pack member, as are you, and that's not going to change. If you can't be nice to him, then I'll have to make sure you're never in the same room, which means one of you will miss family dinners and other things we do together. Is that really what you want?"

It wasn't. James had always been a loner, but he'd been fine because he'd had Chance and Houston. They'd grown up together and had been best friends since they wore diapers. James had always thought nothing would change that, but Wade might.

James couldn't give him that kind of power. He couldn't allow Wade, of all people, to ruin his life.

He got to his feet. "You're right, and I apologize again. I'll just leave for tonight. That way, you can finish dinner in peace."

But of course, Wade had to get everyone's attention back on him. He quickly got up from his seat, almost falling in his haste. "I'll go. I'm tired, anyway. I promise I'll do better."

"Neither of you has to go," Chance said. He sounded tired, and James felt guilty that it was in part because of him.

"It's fine," Wade promised.

He was acting like he was hiding something. James wouldn't be surprised if he was. He suspected Wade was always hiding something, but probably nothing of importance.

Except that maybe, in this case, it could be. James disliked Wade, but it didn't mean he wanted something to happen to the kid. He was important to Theo, which made him important to Chance. Besides, he was a pack member. James had to keep him safe, if anything because of that.

On the other hand, whatever Wade was planning probably wasn't bad. It was no doubt childish, like maybe throwing toilet paper at James's house or something. James would be pissed, but at least it would distract Wade and show Chance that James wasn't the one who always started it. Wade was pretty damn good at antagonizing James, and maybe it was time for people to realize that he wasn't a sweet angel just because he had blond curls and blue eyes. If anything, he was a devil in disguise.

James couldn't allow Wade to draw him deeper into this. He couldn't risk his friendship with Chance, and he couldn't risk his job and the safety of the pack.

Whatever Wade was planning, he was on his own. James would protect him if the pack was attacked, but that was where it ended.

It had to be.

"I don't get it," said one of Theo's brothers who was sitting on James's other side.

James tried to remember the man's name. He knew the

names of all seven people who had arrived with Theo, but sometimes, he wasn't quite sure who was who. He was pretty sure this wasn't Theo's actual brother, Seth, but that wasn't quite as helpful as he wished.

He nodded, intent on ending the conversation before it began, but the guy wouldn't let it go. He leaned closer to James, as if he didn't want anyone else to hear what he had to say.

"Wade is a good guy. He can be a lot sometimes, but that's how he copes. He had to come up with coping mechanisms while we were on the streets, and while I don't think you can understand that, I don't know why you're not giving him a chance. You're willing to listen to everyone else, but not Wade. I know for sure he hasn't done anything to you, so I don't get it."

"There's nothing to explain," James said stiffly. "I already apologized to Chance, but I can apologize to you, too, if you feel I have to."

The man—James was pretty sure his name was Red—rolled his eyes. "You know, I don't understand why you and Wade don't get along. You're both assholes when you want to be."

"I'm nothing like Wade," James snapped. He sucked in a breath, telling himself that the last thing he needed was to start a fight with another of Theo's brothers. "I apologize. Look, I don't have anything against Wade. I just don't like the way he behaves, and while I understand that he's never been part of a pack before, he has to learn."

"He was part of a pack. God, you really *are* an asshole."

James told himself not to feel guilty. "You know that's not what I meant. He was never part of a formal pack, so maybe he doesn't understand how it works. That's fine, and I don't hold it against him, but he needs to start learning. Chance was clear that you would be welcome to stay with us as long as you became productive members of the pack, and I don't feel that Wade is willing to do that."

"That's where you're wrong. You'd see it if you gave Wade a chance, but somehow, I don't think you will, and I don't blame him for snapping at you. I thought he exaggerated, but you truly hate him."

James stiffened. "I don't hate anyone."

It wasn't his fault that Wade was too handsome and sweet when he was with his family. James needed to stay away from him, and Wade hadn't taken the hint, no matter how many times James had told him. James had been fine with the distance between them in the beginning, but Wade had started to push back. That was when James had become an asshole, and while it might not have been the best way to do things, there was no going back now.

He'd antagonized Wade so much that Wade would leave him alone. He hadn't expected the situation to get out of hand, but it had. He needed to stop before Chance decided he couldn't stand it anymore.

And before someone got seriously hurt.

Chapter Three

Wade hated that James got to stay back with his family while he was leaving, but it was the only way for him to be able to get out of pack territory without anyone noticing. If he waited until his family was done with dinner headed back home, he wouldn't have the opportunity to pack a bag and get out. He didn't want to leave, but he felt it was necessary, now more than ever.

He was going to find the mages and show everyone they were wrong.

He stomped through the forest, stumbling on roots and fallen branches. He was letting emotions get to him, which was understandable. He'd never been a hateful kind of person, but James brought out all the bitterness in him, and he didn't understand why.

Maybe it was because when they'd first met, Wade had been amused by how grumpy James was. Back then, he'd thought that James was trying to protect his pack, and it had made sense. Of course he wouldn't want a bunch of strangers to move in with the pack, especially when one of them was sleeping with his alpha. He'd probably believed Theo would try to take over or something stupid like that. It had been amusing but sweet.

Now, Wade knew James was anything but sweet.

He was an asshole who believed he was better than anyone else. He was a stick in the mud, and no one and nothing would ever be able to change that. Wade had stopped trying to, and he was pretty sure that James would never speak to him again after the stunt he was about to pull.

Good.

It would be better for them to stay away from each other. Dinner had been a disaster, and while Wade could admit it had been partly his fault, he wasn't the only one who'd ruined it. James had been right there with him, and Wade couldn't help but wonder if they'd ever be able to fix this. They didn't have to be friends. They didn't even have to be friendly. As long as both of them managed to keep their mouths shut when they were with each other, they could probably make it work.

A branch hit Wade in the face, and he pushed it away, glaring at it as if it were James. James would never keep his mouth shut. He was too full of himself and always happy to tell everyone about his accomplishments. He felt important, and technically, he was. Being head of security was an important job, and James kept everyone in the pack safe, including Wade. That was probably what bothered him so much. He hated Wade and didn't want him to be safe. Hell, he'd probably be happy once he and the others realized that Wade was gone.

Was it too much to ask for James to like him? Wade didn't understand why James hated him so much, and it bothered him. He didn't think anyone had ever hated him like that, and it didn't sit right with him, but he didn't know how to fix it. Not poking at James would be a good start, but Wade wasn't sure he could do that. When he saw James, he wanted nothing more than to prod him until he got a reaction.

Probably because if Wade didn't, James would be ignoring him.

Okay, so Wade wanted James's attention. Maybe it was because James was handsome and strong, and Wade had had a crush on him since he and his family had arrived in Mayport. It didn't make sense, and it wasn't smart, but then feelings often didn't make sense and weren't smart, and crushes were *never* smart. They were just crushes that eventually passed, even though Wade had hoped that he and James could become more than what they were now.

That wouldn't be hard. They were nothing right now except annoyances.

The house was eerily silent, but Wade didn't waste time. He rushed to his bedroom, his brain already working on the problem that Red would eventually come home to sleep and realize Wade wasn't there. If Wade wasn't careful, Red would also see that he'd packed a bag, and then he'd raise the alarm. They'd all come after him, which was the last thing Wade needed. If he was going to do this and show everyone that he could be useful and that he wasn't an idiot, he had to be allowed to reach the clan.

The problem was that he would be on foot. He'd never learned to drive, and he certainly didn't have time to start now. Besides, he couldn't steal one of the cars that belonged to the pack. It would only get him in more trouble. No, it was better to go on foot or hooves, which he planned to do.

So he went back to the porch to grab one of the bags that would go around his neck. He didn't need much, especially if he'd be spending time in his okapi form. Maybe he could sleep that way so he wouldn't have to pay for a motel room. Thankfully, he had money to do so, thanks to Chance and the pack, but he didn't want to abuse their generosity. He still hadn't found a job, which was one of the things that irked James so much.

But Wade would show him.

He changed out of his dressier clothes, opting for an old pair of jeans and a comfortable sweater. He'd take them off soon, but in the meantime, he felt freer than he had in his dress shirt. It was easier to move, especially since he stayed barefoot. He remembered to put his shoes into his bag, along with a few changes of clothes, his toothbrush, and other things.

No one was home yet by the time he was done packing, so he quickly headed to the back door. That way, they wouldn't see him if they came back while he was still here.

He hadn't counted on anyone coming home early, but he should have. When he stepped on the back porch, he almost had a heart attack at the sight of Red sitting on a bench. He hadn't been here earlier, but he'd seen Wade, so it was too late now.

"What are you doing?" he asked, his gaze raking over Wade's body. It stopped on the bag in Wade's hands, and he got to his feet. "Please tell me you're not running away because of James."

Wade snorted. "As if I'd give him the satisfaction. No, I'm here to stay, and he'll have to learn to deal with that."

Red snickered. "Good. I've never known you to walk away from a challenge, and I'm glad to find out you're not gonna start now." His expression sobered up. "But you're up to something, and I don't like it. What's going on?"

"I'm going to find Dustin's brother."

Red groaned. "That's not a good idea, Wade."

"Probably not, but I'm the only one willing to do it."

"You can't blame Chance for not wanting to put any of his pack members in danger."

"I don't. I understand where he's coming from. I don't like that no one is taking this seriously, though. The mages decimated the clan, and they probably kidnapped Dustin's brother. Who's to say they won't do the same to us? Can we hide our heads in the sand just because they haven't targeted us yet?"

"I get what you're saying, but you should talk to Chance, not go on your own. You're not trained to fight, and you shouldn't put yourself in danger."

Wade knew Red was worried about him. He'd be worried

if any of his family members were planning on doing this, too. He was convinced of what he was doing, though, and he had no intention of allowing anyone to stop him.

"I'll be fine," he promised. "I'm not going to try to take on an entire mage coven by myself. I'm not an idiot." Even though James seemed to think he was. "I just want to talk to Dustin's father and maybe find out where the mages are staying. I know I won't be able to get Dustin's brother on my own, but maybe if I have more info, it'll convince Chance to help." And if the alpha still didn't change his mind, well, Wade would have to find a way to get Mark out. He was scrappy, and he always got himself out of trouble.

This time wouldn't be any different.

James was relieved when dinner was finally over. Things had stayed tense after Wade had left, and he couldn't blame anyone who'd been there. They were family, yet James and Wade didn't behave that way. They behaved like enemies and were constantly at each other's throats, and James could admit how draining it was on the others.

It was draining for him, too. It wasn't that he wanted to fight with Wade. He just found Wade annoying, and it was fun to get a rise out of him when he was usually so laid back.

James stopped dead in his tracks in the middle of the trees on his way home.

Shit. Was what Chance had said earlier correct? Was this James's version of pulling Wade's pigtails?

It couldn't be. James didn't like Wade, and besides, Chance was right. Hurting someone that way, even as a child, wasn't right. It was an excuse that adults made, but James couldn't do that. He had to be honest.

He would never hurt Wade physically. He couldn't imagine raising a hand to him, and when he forced himself to try, it made him feel sick. Yes, it was fun to mess with Wade, but it was also fun to have Wade mess with him, at least until things went too far and they got angry. That was when things got out of hand, and James had no idea how to stop it from happening.

There was no way he liked Wade. Wade was an annoying little shit, and James could think of nothing worse than spending the rest of his life with him.

Yet his chest felt tight and warm when he thought about that.

He started walking again, but he decided not to head home. He wouldn't be able to sleep anyway, so he might as well patrol the area to make sure everyone was fine and back where they belonged.

Chance and Theo, along with Theo's family, had been annoyed with him earlier. They'd barely said goodbye, and James knew it was entirely his fault. Wade might be a little shit, but James was an asshole, and he was very much aware of that. It had served him well when it came to doing his job, but it was becoming a problem in his personal life. He didn't want to lose a friend because he couldn't be nice to Wade. Maybe tomorrow morning, he should apologize. The thought made him want to throw up, mostly because Wade would be incredibly smug, but something was going to break if they didn't stop behaving like this.

A branch cracking got his attention. He looked around, but for a few seconds he saw nothing but trees. He could hear a small animal scurrying close to him, but that wasn't what had stepped on the branch. No, that had to be something bigger, and while it was probably a pack member, James wasn't willing to risk it.

He snuck around the trees in the direction of the noise. As he moved closer, he could hear footsteps, then someone grumbling to themselves. He thought he recognized the voice of one of Wade's brothers, so he wasn't overly worried.

The problem was that the guy wasn't headed to his own home. He was headed back to Chance and Theo's house, and James didn't want them to be woken up for nothing. If there was a problem, he'd take care of it.

"What are you doing?" he asked as he finally reached the guy.

Red squeaked and jumped back. One second, he was there, and the next, he'd vanished.

Well, not vanished. James looked down to see a bundle still dressed in Red's clothes. He didn't have arms and legs anymore and was kind of round. James didn't know for sure what kind of animal Red and the others could shift into, except for Wade.

Everyone knew that Wade was an Okapi shifter because he never shut up about it.

James crouched next to Red and gently poked at the round thing. "Hey, it's okay. I'm sorry I startled you, but I was wondering what you are doing in the forest on your own this late at night. I thought everyone had gone home."

There was a rustle, and a small nose appeared from under Red's sweater. James watched as a long face emerged, quickly followed by the rest of Red's body.

He was an armadillo shifter.

James wanted to feel how hard Red's back was, but he didn't dare. He wouldn't have appreciated it if someone had tried touching him in his bear form without asking, and he and Red weren't friends.

He got to his feet and took a step back, giving Red space to shift back. He did, not looking at James as he quickly got dressed again. Thankfully, his animal form was small, so he hadn't torn anything.

"I was going back to Chance's house. Wade's up to something, and I need to tell him."

James snorted. "When is Wade *not* up to something?"

"You're not wrong."

Hopefully the smile playing on Red's lips meant he wasn't angry at James. James didn't have anything against Theo's family except for Wade. He still wasn't sure that welcoming them into the Mayport pack had been such a great idea, but there was no going back, and he had to learn to live with that.

"But this is different. He packed a bag and left," Red continued.

Shock froze James's body for a second. Red's words didn't make sense. Wade was like a barnacle. Once he'd latched on, he wasn't letting go, which applied to everything as far as James had seen. "Why?" It didn't make sense.

Had he left because of James? Did he feel like he didn't have a place with the pack because of how James treated him?

That wasn't what James intended. To be fair, he didn't know what he'd wanted, but not that. He would never take the pack and Wade's family away from Wade, no matter how much he disliked him.

"He said he wanted to find Dustin's brother and the mages."

Of course he did. James should have known that was his reason instead of worrying about having pushed Wade to run. He wasn't doing this because he was sad that James couldn't accept him. He was doing it because he wanted to show everyone that he was right—the asshole.

"How long ago did he leave?" James needed to know if he was going to catch up to him.

"Five minutes, maybe? I wasn't sure I should tell Theo and Chance, and Wade made me promise I wouldn't, but what if he gets hurt? He said that maybe the mages would move on to the Mayport pack now that they're done with the dragons, and he might not be wrong. If he goes there, they could hurt him, and I'd never forgive myself if something happened to him and I could have stopped it."

"All right. You go to Chance's house and tell him and Theo what's going on. I'll go after Wade and drag his ass back to pack territory."

"Why would you do that? You hate him, so I thought you'd be happy he's gone."

James had always been an asshole, and usually, he didn't care. He didn't want Red and the others to think he was so evil that he wouldn't go after Wade. "It doesn't matter if I like or dislike him. He's a pack member, so I'm responsible for keeping him safe."

"Even though some days, you want to strangle him?"

James almost laughed. "You mean most days, right? Yes. No matter what, he's a pack member, and that means everything. Go tell Theo and Chance. I'll bring Wade back, but they need to know what's happening."

James turned his head and sniffed the air. He could tell which direction Wade had taken even in his human form, but that wouldn't be enough. He had to shift, and he had to do it quickly. Otherwise, he would lose Wade's trail.

Even if he did, it wouldn't be a problem. James knew where Wade was headed, so he'd find him even if he couldn't catch up to him.

Wade wasn't an idiot, and he knew his family. Red had promised he wouldn't tell anyone, but he would. As soon as he had a few minutes to wrap his mind around what Wade had told him and realize that Wade could be in danger, he'd break his promise, and since he couldn't stop Wade anymore, he'd go to someone who could.

Chance.

Wade didn't like the thought of disappointing his new alpha, much less disappointing Theo's boyfriend. Chance had been nothing but nice since Wade had arrived in Mayport, and Wade hoped that wouldn't change after tonight.

Chance would be angry. He'd be right to feel that way, and Wade was ready to let the alpha yell at him for however long he felt was necessary. He was doing the right thing, even though he was putting himself in danger.

Maybe he should have mentioned earlier that the mages might move on to Mayport now that they were done with the dragon clan, but he hadn't thought about it. He also believed it probably wouldn't happen, if anything because the clan wasn't close enough to pack territory. There were several other groups of shifters between them, and if anything happened to them, the pack would find out. They could get ready for the mages, although Wade wasn't quite sure how.

Mages fought with magic. It had enabled them to create shifters and probably made it possible for them to block all the dragons in Dustin's old clan from shifting. What possibility would the pack have if the mages did the same to them?

They needed to find out more about the mages, and even more importantly, they needed to find Mark. Though Wade had never met the guy, Dustin shared that his brother was distant, but he'd always been there for Dustin. He'd tried to stop their father from marrying Dustin off to seal an alliance with another clan, and while he hadn't done enough when Dustin had been taken, he cared. Dustin cared about Mark, too, and Wade wanted him to be happy.

He stretched out his neck and ran faster. It was getting harder now that he wasn't in pack territory anymore. There was no one to clean up the forest and keep the paths clear, but that didn't matter. Running made Wade feel free, and right now, he was.

Freedom was an odd thing. Technically, Wade had been free for most of his recent life. He'd been living on the streets with no one to tell him what to do except for Theo, but Wade had been the one who decided to allow Theo to do that. He and the others had known they needed a leader, and Theo had made the most sense.

But that hadn't been freedom. They'd been forced into it, and they'd used most of their energy to survive. Sure, they'd been free to do whatever they wanted with their day and to move all over the country, but at what cost? It hadn't been freedom. Wade was glad it was over.

Was he free with the pack? In a way, he was. Chance would never force him to do anything he didn't want. He was a good alpha, as well as Theo's boyfriend. But he expected things from Wade, so Wade was once again restricted.

But it didn't matter. He didn't need freedom if it meant being away from his family and starving. He was perfectly happy with the Mayport pack and had no intention of leaving it anytime soon.

Besides, real freedom was this. He ran through the night, his hooves hitting the ground hard, raising puffs of dust he could see in the moonlight. The forest around him welcomed him and made him feel part of it. He had to be careful and skirt a few territories he didn't want to encroach on, but he'd studied the place where Dustin had grown up on a map. He knew how to get there and which areas to avoid, and while it meant he'd have to run for most of the night, it wasn't a problem. He knew what he was doing, and the world around him was silent and asleep.

So he ran. He couldn't remember the last time he'd run so much and for so long, but it had been a while, and by the time he reached the outskirts of the small town where Dustin had lived, he was exhausted. He was tempted to lie down and go to sleep as he was, but he was afraid someone might notice him. What if they didn't realize he was a shifter and thought he was just a strange deer? Would they try hunting him? He couldn't risk it, which meant he didn't have a choice. He needed to get a room somewhere, at least for the night, but possibly for longer. He wouldn't be lucky enough to find the mages and Mark on the first try.

No, it would probably take days, and he'd need a place to call home during those days. He might as well get the room for a week.

But this wasn't his home. The Mayport pack was, and he couldn't wait to go back.

His skin itched as he shifted back to his human form, but it was from the sweat rather than from the feeling of being away from the only place where he belonged.

He didn't know anything about this town except that it was where Dustin had grown up. Tomorrow would be a day of exploring and talking to people, and hopefully he would find out where the mages were, or at the very least, if people had noticed anything odd happening recently. He was curious to find out if anyone shared his opinion about mages, but he couldn't ask. He needed people to talk to him, not think he was an idiot.

As he got dressed, his thoughts drifted back to James. He'd be so pissed when he found out Wade was gone, and it was kind of a pity that Wade wouldn't be there to see him. Would his face go red? It always did when James was angry, and Wade often expected James's head to explode.

More likely, he wouldn't care. Hell, he'd probably throw a party when he found out. That was how much he hated Wade.

Luckily for Wade, it was fairly easy to find a motel. There were two next to each other, which felt like a lot considering how small the town was, but Wade shrugged it off. He headed to the first one, relieved to see someone sitting behind the office desk. The door was closed, so he knocked, and the woman's head shot up. She looked wary, probably because it was late at night, but she still got up to let him in.

"I'm sorry to bother you," Wade said, using his best smile.

It usually got him what he wanted, and more importantly, it made him look harmless. There were times when he hated his blond hair and blue eyes, especially paired with his short height, but in situations like this one, they were a good way to make people feel at ease with him.

This woman wasn't any different. Her shoulders relaxed, and she gestured for him to approach the desk.

"No worries. It's what we're here for."

"Do you think I could get a room for a week?"

"We can do that," she confirmed.

Wade allowed himself to relax, too. Technically, he was in enemy territory, and the dragons could attack him at any second. The woman was human, so she probably wouldn't run to Dustin's father to tell him about Wade. Besides, what would she tell him? That a stranger was getting a room in her motel? Wasn't that the point of owning a motel?

Wade would deal with all of this tomorrow morning. For now, he took the key the woman offered, paid what he owed her, and trudged his way to his room.

He needed to sleep, and hopefully, in the morning, he'd still be in one piece and wouldn't have become dragon kibble.

James was pissed. That seemed to be his usual emotion when he was dealing with Wade, but today took the cake. When he got his hands on Wade, he was going to strangle him, dammit.

What was he thinking? Why was he throwing himself into danger like that? Yes, he cared about Dustin and wanted his friend to get his brother back, but most people wouldn't have decided to do all of this on their own.

But Wade had, and James could only imagine how Dustin's father would react when he found out Wade was in town.

If James found Wade in one piece, it would be a miracle.

He'd been trying to catch up to Wade since they left pack

territory, but Wade was faster. Not that bear shifters weren't fast, but not nearly as much as an okapi shifter, and James especially had always been slower and bulkier. That meant he didn't reach Wade in time to get him back to pack territory, and the only thing he could do was follow Wade's scent.

His phone vibrated again in the bag around his neck. It had been doing that often, and James knew it was either Chance or Houston. They wanted to know what was going on and what James was up to, but right now, he was busy.

Besides, how could he answer that question? He didn't know what he was up to. He just knew that Wade was a pack member and that he needed to keep him safe.

And that was all there was to it. It had to be all there was to it.

The thought of something happening to Wade made James want to throw up. No matter how much he disliked the other man, he didn't want him to die. Besides, he wasn't entirely sure he disliked him. Wade was annoying, but there was more to him than that. When he annoyed James, he never said anything that wasn't true. Even tonight, he hadn't, and James knew himself enough to admit that.

He was an asshole. He was too focused on his job, and it made sense that no one wanted to be in a relationship with him. Luckily, that was fine with him, but Wade clearly didn't understand. He wanted to be loved, like most people.

James didn't care about that, or at least that was what he told himself. He didn't need to be loved. He just needed to be allowed to do his job, and in this case, his job was dragging Wade back to pack territory. Well, not literally, because it would get people's attention if he dragged Wade back in the middle of the day. He had no doubt Wade would make a mess out of the situation.

But that wouldn't stop him from trying.

He followed Wade's trail to a spot at the edge of the town

where Dustin had grown up. It didn't look like much, especially in the early hours of the morning. The town was asleep, and everything was dark.

Everything but the two motels James could see from this position. There was a single room lit—probably the office—and James knew that was where Wade had gone. He didn't need to sniff the air to find Wade's scent, but he did anyway.

Sure enough, it headed toward one of the motels. James was careful as he followed it, not wanting anyone to see him in his bear form. They'd freak out and raise the alarm, and this mess would become even bigger. He might be okay dealing with Wade because Wade was a pack member, but he didn't want anything to do with the dragons or the people who lived in this town.

He slipped his way closer to the motel. He could smell that Wade had headed into the office, which meant he'd probably gotten a room. James ignored the office and sniffed until he found Wade's scent again. Then he followed it to a closed door.

He listened for a moment, pressing his furry body against the door. Everything inside was silent, as if Wade had already fallen asleep. He had to be exhausted. James was, and he couldn't wait to face-plant in the nearest bed.

Except that the nearest bed was Wade's, and there was no way James was going there.

But now that he knew where Wade was, he could relax for a few hours. He hid behind a dumpster and shifted, then quickly dressed. His phone wasn't vibrating anymore, but he winced when he saw that he had six missed calls and more than a dozen text messages. He made his way to the office, eager to get all of this over with.

The woman in the office appeared a little puzzled, probably because two strangers had asked for a room almost simultaneously. James didn't imagine that she often had that many people, and he hoped she wasn't a dragon and wouldn't contact Dustin's father to tell him what was going on.

He asked for the room next to Wade's, and the woman was happy to give it to him. He didn't pause by Wade's door again. He headed straight into his room, wrinkling his nose at the strong scent of bleach. At least it was clean.

As soon as he was inside, he closed the door and took out his phone. He dialed Chance's number, steeling himself for what was about to happen.

"What the fuck were you thinking?" Chance asked when he answered.

"That I couldn't let him go on his own. I tried to catch up to him, but he was too fast. What was I supposed to do? Let him go?"

"Come to me instead of sending Red."

"I had to act in the moment." James rubbed his face. "Look, I'm sorry if I disappointed you. I honestly didn't mean to and thought I was doing the right thing. I didn't want Wade to get hurt."

"Why not? You hate him."

James winced. He didn't like that everyone believed he hated Wade—he didn't. He just didn't like him much. "He's a pack member, and my job is to protect all pack members. It's why I'm here. I couldn't let him go alone, and there was no time to get anyone else. Can I call you back in the morning? Because I ran for most of the night, and I'm exhausted."

Chance sighed. "Call me as soon as you wake up. I want to know what's going on."

"Do you want me to drag Wade back home? You know he won't be happy." James could imagine the kind of hell Wade would raise if he tried, but if that was what his alpha wished for, he'd do it.

"Just talk to him, all right? I understand why he's doing

this, and I don't blame him. Something needs to be done, and I should have stepped up."

"You're protecting your pack."

"Maybe so, but I might also be putting it in danger. We'll talk about it tomorrow."

James wanted to insist that Chance had done the right thing, but he couldn't. Chance wouldn't listen to him, not right now. They were both tired, and James especially needed sleep if he was going to deal with Wade tomorrow morning.

There was no way out of it.

He set his phone to wake him early. He needed time to call Chance again before getting to Wade. They had to talk about what they'd do with Wade and his stupid mission of finding mages. They weren't real, so he'd be here poking around for the rest of his life if that was what he wanted to find.

But it wasn't the only thing he was here for. Wade wanted to save Dustin's brother, and James couldn't find it in himself to hold that against him. If Chance's or Houston's brother had been missing, James would do anything he could to get them back.

That was what family did.

Chapter Four

When Wade's phone alarm went off, he wished he could chuck it out the window. It was way too early, especially after running most of the night, and he was exhausted. His body felt stiff, and he briefly wondered if he'd be able to walk without looking like an eighty-year-old.

There was only one way to find out.

He groaned and slapped at the stupid phone. He was tempted to turn it off entirely, but he knew his family would be calling, and they'd freak out if they couldn't reach him.

That didn't mean he'd answer them. He was planning on sending a group text to tell them he was okay, then he'd ignore them as long as he was working.

Because yes, he had work to do.

He headed to the bathroom to take a shower, taking his time as he thought about what his next move would be. He'd talked to Dustin about his family, so he knew where to find Dustin's father. Apparently, the man spent a lot of time at the local diner. Dustin didn't know if things had changed since the clan had been attacked, but that would be the best place for Wade to start. If Dustin's father wasn't there, he'd look around town and start asking questions. He wasn't sure people would answer, but he had to at least try.

He didn't know how else to find the mages. Hopefully someone had noticed something—anything. He just needed some clues to point him in the right direction.

He had so many problems he couldn't even start thinking about them. Of course he needed to find out where the mages were, but what would he do if he did? He couldn't exactly fight them on his own, but that didn't mean he was giving up on finding Mark. Mark was probably in pain if the mages had him, and Wade couldn't risk waiting too long. Dustin's brother could die, and that would destroy Dustin. Wade didn't even want to contemplate that possibility. Besides, he'd just started. He'd find what he needed, and when he did, he'd go home and show Chance and everyone else that he was right. Hopefully, the pack would finally agree to step in. Maybe if they knew Mark's location and what was happening to him, they'd be more willing to help.

Wade washed his hair and his weary body, and by the time he was done, he felt more awake. He still wasn't awake enough to do much without coffee, but since he was headed to the diner, he'd be able to get some there. Thankfully, Chance had made sure every member of their family had money they could spend, even though most of them weren't working yet. It meant Wade would be able to pay for his motel room and food while he was here. It also meant Chance would be able to see where Wade was, but that wasn't a secret anyway, so it didn't matter.

Wade doubted Chance would attempt to drag him home. He cared about his pack members and wanted to protect them, but he didn't clip their wings, and as far as Wade was concerned, it was one of the reasons he was such a good alpha.

Once Wade was dry and dressed in the clean clothes he'd packed into the bag, it was time to head out the door. He grabbed the key, his cell phone, and his wallet and went to open the door.

Only to freeze.

James was standing in front of the door, leaning against a car parked there. Wade didn't recognize it, so it probably wasn't James's.

Was the weirdo leaning against a car that wasn't his?

"What are you doing here?" he asked. He didn't wait for James to answer. Instead, he turned to lock his door, acting as if he didn't care that James was there.

He truly didn't, at least not beyond the fact that James might be here to take him home. If so, he wouldn't go easily, and he'd make sure James paid for what he was doing.

The man hated his guts. Why would he care where Wade was and what he was doing? Why would he be here to take him home? He wouldn't be here of his own volition, so it had to mean that Chance had asked him to come.

The bottom of Wade's stomach dropped. If Chance had asked James to come, then he was pissed and wanted Wade to come home so he could yell at him. Wade had never heard of Chance hurting any of his pack members, but he hadn't been in Mayport for long. What if Chance decided to make Wade pay?

But why would he? Why would he care if something happened to Wade? Wade hadn't been a pack member for long, so most people wouldn't even notice he was gone. There was no way Chance cared that much about Wade yet, so why would it matter to him?

Maybe not to him, but it would matter to Theo. Maybe that was why Chance wanted to make sure Wade was all right.

James appeared relaxed, but something told Wade he wasn't. Wade tried to ignore him, but it wasn't easy. The man was glaring a hole in the back of Wade's head, and it became even more obvious when Wade turned to face the asshole.

"What the fuck were you thinking?" James asked, pushing away from the car. "Running away like that in the middle of the night. Are you an idiot? What did you think was going to happen?"

Wade shrugged. "Nothing. And you know what? That's what happened. I arrived without trouble, and I'm perfectly fine. Nothing happened to me, and nothing is going to happen." He tried to sound convinced, but he doubted James would leave. If he was here, he had a reason, and he wouldn't leave until he got what he wanted.

"You could have gotten killed."

"Well, I wasn't, so you can call Chance and tell him that."

He turned to walk toward the street. He'd looked at the map before leaving his room, so he knew the general direction he needed to take.

He'd hoped James would understand that he needed to stay back, but he wasn't that lucky.

James came after him, still talking as he followed. "You're a Mayport pack member now. That means you can't just go off the way you did. You need to go back, and you need to do it now."

"So what? Because I'm a pack member, I can't leave pack territory?" Wade asked.

"That's not what I meant. We're not prisoners in pack territory."

"Then I don't see what the problem is. If pack members are free to leave, which is what I did, everything's fine, right? You don't have a reason to be here, so you can go home."

Wade could see the diner in the distance. His stomach churned and gurgled with nervousness and hunger. James's presence wasn't helping, and it took everything Wade had not to punch him in his smug face.

Really, *why* was James here? Why hadn't Chance sent someone else? It would have made more sense. Chance had to know there was no way Wade would come back with James, of all people. And why hadn't James refused? He didn't want to be here anymore than Wade wanted him to be.

"You're not listening to me," James said with a growl. He grabbed Wade's arm, and both of them froze.

"Let go," Wade said through gritted teeth.

Thankfully, James obeyed. There was no way he was afraid of Wade, but he seemed to realize he'd done something wrong. He raised both his hands as if he expected Wade to be afraid of him.

As if Wade could ever be afraid of him.

"I'm just trying to make you see sense," James said. "You're putting yourself in danger for no good reason. We don't know how Dustin's father is going to react to having you here, but it won't be good. Do you want to become dragon food? Because that's what's going to happen to you if you don't stop this madness."

Wade glared. "Dustin's father isn't going to attack me. I'm not going to talk to him when he's alone, because I'm not a complete idiot." Wade swallowed. "Even though you believe I am, and you're not the only one. No one believed me, not even Chance, but I'll show you. I'll find the mages, and I'll take Mark home." Even if he had to die to make that happen.

And he just might have to.

Wade was a fucking idiot. James didn't understand how he couldn't see what was right before him, but maybe he did. Maybe he just was so stubborn that he couldn't admit he was wrong.

James wasn't sure what to do. He'd expected Wade to be sheepish and follow him home without arguing. He should have known better, but he'd fooled himself into believing he'd be home soon. Wade had always been a troublemaker. That meant he wasn't going anywhere unless James dragged him there, and he couldn't very well do that in the middle of the street.

There weren't that many people around, but the few people they walked past stared at them. It was clear they were strangers. Everyone knew everyone in such a small town, and

Wade and James stuck out like a sore thumb.

Wade seemed to know where he was going, which meant he'd talked to Dustin about his father. James didn't understand why Dustin had told Wade anything. This seemed like a particularly bad idea, especially after what had happened to the clan. Dustin's father was convinced that the Mayport pack had something to do with the attack, and he wouldn't take finding two pack members on his doorstep nicely.

James shouldn't have touched Wade earlier, and he still shouldn't touch him now, but it was the only way to make him stop. He reached for him again, intent on dragging him into an alley or a quiet spot where they could talk, but Wade saw him move. He ducked out of the way and stuck out his tongue, and by the time James was done sputtering, he'd opened the diner door.

James had no choice but to follow him inside. He was on high alert, looking around and trying to find the shifters in the room. He should have been able to smell them, but the scent of dragon shifter was heavy in the diner. It had to be a place where they often gathered, which would make things more difficult. James was trained to fight, and as a bear shifter, he was bigger than most other shifters, but he wasn't bigger than a dragon. He doubted he'd be able to take one on in a fight, let alone several of them. His only hope was that they wouldn't dare shift in the diner, since he could smell humans, too.

"There he is," Wade said.

He made a beeline for an older man sitting in a booth at the back of the diner. He was next to the kitchen door, sipping on a cup of coffee and staring at his phone. He looked harmless, but James knew that wasn't true when he looked up.

The man's gaze was hard, and it was clear he wouldn't hesitate to smack Wade down if he didn't like whatever Wade was about to do. James suspected that was quite likely, so he rushed forward.

That didn't mean he liked Wade. He was doing this because Wade was a pack member, nothing more.

"You're Dustin's father," Wade announced when he reached the man's table.

Dustin's father looked him up and down. "What the fuck do you want?"

Wade was smart enough not to offer the man his hand.

James was pretty sure the alpha would have bitten it off or something.

"Alpha Wilson, my name is Wade. I'm a friend of Dustin's."

Alpha Wilson growled. "Don't call me alpha. I don't have a clan anymore."

"I'm sorry about that. Do you have any news of your son?"

"Didn't you just say you were Dustin's friend? Shouldn't you know where he is?"

"I meant Mark. Dustin is worried about his brother."

Wilson took a sip of his coffee. "Well, he shouldn't be. Mark is dead."

James heard Wade suck in a breath. He wasn't sure what made him do it, but he gently pressed a hand against Wade's back. He expected Wade to step away, but instead, he leaned into the touch and straightened his back.

"Have you seen his body?"

"I don't need to see his body to know he's dead. He would have come home if he was still alive, but I haven't heard from him since the attack." Wilson narrowed his eyes. "You said you're Dustin's friend. Are you part of his new pack?"

That was a dangerous question, and James prayed Wade wouldn't answer.

So of course, Wade did.

"I lived with him on the streets when he was homeless. I've been part of his new family since he left home."

Wilson snorted. "Family."

"Yes, family. You don't have to like me being here, and you don't have to like Dustin, but why aren't you looking for Mark? He's your son and heir, and you should be tearing apart this entire area to get to him."

Wilson slammed a hand on the table. Wade jumped and took a step closer to James, and James stood strong behind him. He glared at Wilson, but Wilson didn't even seem to see him. He was focused on Wade.

"You don't get to come here and tell me what to do," Wilson snarled. "If you want to look for Mark, then be my guest, but you'll only find his body. All of this is useless. The clan is gone, as are my sons. I don't have anything left, and it's all your fault. I know the Mayport pack was behind this. I know Dustin is the reason the clan is gone."

James already knew Wade wouldn't let that pass. He wasn't surprised when Wade surged forward, but he hooked his finger around Wade's belt to keep him back. It wouldn't do anyone any good if Wade started a physical fight with Wilson, although it would be funny. Wade looked fragile and innocent, but James already knew that he had a spine of steel and wouldn't hesitate to stand up to Wilson, even if it earned him bruises.

"Dustin had nothing to do with this, and he's worried sick about Mark," Wade spat out. "As for the attack, the Mayport pack didn't have anything to do with it. How would we have stopped you from shifting? No shifter can do something like that, but you know who can? Mages."

Wilson stared at Wade for a second. Then he started laughing and leaned back in his seat.

Wade looked like he wanted to scratch Wilson's eyes out. James was tempted to let him go just to see how that went, but Chance would kick his ass if Wade had as much as a bruise on him when he came home.

"You're nothing more than a child," Wilson said. There was still humor in his voice. "Mages. How did you come up with that? Have you been reading stories?"

Wade pushed forward, and James hauled him back. The fact that Wade didn't even turn to glare at him meant he was entirely focused on Wilson, which was never a good thing. Wade's focus meant chaos.

"I might be young, but you have to admit that your clan wasn't able to shift, and that there's no way shifters can make that happen. How do you think it did, then? What do you think happened?"

Wilson shrugged. He was trying to act as if he didn't care, but he'd been an alpha. Even though he was a dick, he had to be hurt by the loss of his clan and his people. James found himself feeling almost sorry for him, although that didn't last long.

"It doesn't matter anymore, does it? My clan is gone, and I lost my sons."

"You don't have to have lost them. Look for Mark. Reach out to Dustin."

"My sons are dead." Wilson stared Wade in the eyes. "You can tell Dustin that the next time you see him. He's not my son anymore."

Wade looked hurt, even though he wasn't Dustin. It was time to leave, but James was pretty sure Wade would kick him in the balls if he tried pulling him away.

"Let's go," he whispered instead. "He's not going to help us."

"There's nothing to help you with," Wilson said. "Let it go."

Wade was visibly disappointed, but James knew he never let life push him down for long, and this situation wasn't any different. He'd stood up to Dustin's father, and James's stomach churned. Wade never knew when to stop, even when he was in danger.

Wade wasn't leaving without at least some answers. He didn't care how Dustin's father felt about his sons. He didn't matter anymore, and maybe he never had.

Wilson had been strong when he'd had his clan behind him. He'd been trying to use Dustin to ally with another clan, and it would have made him even stronger. But all of that was gone. Wilson's clan was gone, and while he was a dangerous man, Wade was confident that he wouldn't hurt him. They were in a public place, and there were humans present. Wilson wouldn't risk losing what little he had left.

"Tell me what happened that night," Wade ordered.

Wilson stared at him for a moment. Wade expected him to tell him to fuck off, and he was ready to fight him.

Well, not physically. Even though Wilson was at least twice Wade's age, Wade was pretty sure he'd lose if things came to that. That didn't mean he wouldn't fight to get the answers he needed. It was just that if Wilson turned physical, Wade would push James in front of him.

But Wilson didn't try to hurt Wade. He slumped back in his seat, and suddenly, he looked older. Wade didn't know how old he was, but considering Dustin and Mark's age, Wade would be surprised if he wasn't in his sixties. Right now, though, he looked like he was in his seventies, if not eighties. The attack had aged him, and while he'd been good at hiding it, Wade could see the cracks now.

"What do you want from me?" Wilson asked. "I don't know what happened that night. I was in bed, like every other clan member. There was an explosion, and I ran outside to see what was happening. I tried to shift, but I couldn't. No one could, not even my enforcers. There were people there, and all of them were wearing masks. They killed most of my pack.

I lost sight of Mark in the fight and couldn't find him again."

Wade was excited, but he tried not to let it show. He was *finally* getting answers. "Tell me about the people with the masks. Did they shift?"

"No. They never did."

Wilson was going to make this hard, wasn't he? Why was he withholding information? Why couldn't he see how important this was? If Wilson was trying to hide that he hadn't tried to defend his people, Wade was going to strangle him. He didn't care about how this made Wilson look. He just cared about what had happened and the answers he could get.

"How were they dressed? What did the masks look like? How did they kill so many dragons if they never shifted?"

Wilson looked like he wanted to give Wade a good shake, but he didn't move.

"They were all dressed in black, including the masks. They killed us using knives, and I think I even saw a sword."

"Magic?"

Wilson snorted. "Magic isn't real, boy."

"It looks to me like it is," Wade snapped. "Because it's the reason your dragons weren't able to shift. How did you feel when you tried?"

"Like my dragon was gone. There was just emptiness where he used to be."

Wilson's voice was soft, and there was so much pain in it that Wade almost felt sorry for him.

"Does it still feel that way?" he asked, keeping his tone gentle even though Wilson didn't deserve it. Wade couldn't imagine anything worse than not being able to feel his okapi, so he felt for the guy, even though he was a dick.

Wilson glared at him. "I haven't been able to shift since the attack, and I know that the few survivors are in the same place. Are you done with your questions? Because I don't have anything else to tell you. Leave me alone."

Wade could tell he wouldn't get anything else, so he nodded and turned. James seemed surprised to see him let go so easily, but thankfully, he didn't ask questions. He followed Wade outside, his gaze feeling heavy on Wade's back.

As soon as they were on the sidewalk, Wade's stomach growled. He glared down at it because there was no way he was going back inside. He'd need to find another place to get breakfast, and it had to be soon before his body started to digest itself.

But of course, James had other plans. He grabbed Wade's arm again and pulled him toward the back of the diner. They ended up in a mostly empty parking lot, and James pushed Wade against the nearest wall.

Wade arched a brow. "I don't think that having sex against the wall in the parking lot is a good idea."

James gaped, but it only took him a second to gather himself, which was a pity.

"Shut the fuck up," he snapped. "What do you think you're doing? Why are you antagonizing Wilson? He's going to have you killed, and I can't do anything against a dragon shifter."

"You were next to me when we were talking, so you should remember that Wilson said he hasn't been able to shift since the attack. Or maybe you're going deaf in your old age? You *are* almost forty, after all."

James's face turned red. "You don't know what you're talking about."

"It looks to me like you don't, either." Wade was having fun, but from the previous times they'd done this, he knew it wouldn't last long. They'd soon start yelling at each other, and he couldn't afford for that to happen. He wasn't here to fight with James. He was here to find Mark and find out about mages.

He sighed. "Look, can you let it go? Wilson isn't going to

attack me or anyone else because he can't. He doesn't have the clan anymore, and he can't shift. He's powerless, and he knows it. Don't you think that if he wasn't, he would have kicked me out of the diner?"

Wade pushed away from the wall and tried to walk around James, but James wasn't having it. He grabbed Wade's shoulder and slammed it against the wall, which made Wade squeak.

"That hurt, asshole," Wade snapped.

"You better get used to the pain, because you're going to be in an ocean of it if you don't stop this foolishness. You have to admit the truth, Wade. There are no mages. Mark is dead, and you can't bring him back to Dustin."

Wade tried pushing James away, but the man was twice his size. He didn't budge. "Didn't you hear Wilson? The people who attacked the clan never shifted. They killed the dragons with blades, and they were able to do so only because none of them could shift. Who else could it be? If not mages, who?"

"I don't know."

Wade didn't know how to get through to James. "Do you hate me that much that you're unwilling to even consider that I might be right?" he asked. He sounded desperate, and he was. He didn't know what to do or how to convince people that he wasn't an idiot.

No one remembered mages, but that didn't mean they weren't real. It didn't mean they hadn't attacked the clan or that they hadn't captured Mark. *Mark* was the most important thing in this situation. He was Dustin's brother, and Dustin was hurting. Wade would be all over the place if his sister was missing, which was why he understood. Dustin needed Mark to be okay, which meant they had to find him.

"Look, let's ignore the mages for a moment," he said. He needed to convince James to help. He didn't like him, but

James had more experience. He could probably find out what happened to Mark without too many problems, while it would take Wade days, if not longer. "Mark is missing. He could be dead like his father believes, but what if he's not? What if he's alive and being hurt, and we could do something to help him? Can you live with the knowledge that you might have saved him if you'd just listened to me?"

James stared at Wade without answering.

Wade didn't know what else to do or say. He stared back, hoping against all odds that James wasn't as much of an asshole as he'd been until now.

He expected James to tell him to fuck off or maybe to grab him and drag him back to the motel. He thought that maybe James would ignore him and demand he come home, or else he wouldn't be a Mayport pack member anymore.

But that wasn't what James did. No, what James did was the most shocking thing that could have happened.

He kissed Wade.

James didn't know what he'd been thinking. Actually, he didn't think he'd been thinking at all.

Wade had been talking about Mark and how important he was to Dustin, and it had reminded James of Houston and Chance. If one of them were in Mark's place, he'd be shaking the sky and the earth to find them. He wouldn't stop for anything, not even someone telling him he was an idiot for hoping they were all right.

Mark wasn't Wade's brother, but he was Dustin's, and Wade loved Dustin. Clearly, he was ready to do anything to make Dustin happy. He'd put himself in danger by running away in the middle of the night and facing Dustin's father, and for now, he was still in one piece.

James wanted things to stay that way.

Wade might be a mouthy smart-ass, but he was also caring and warm. He was putting himself in danger for someone he didn't even know, all because it would make one of the people that he considered family happy. How could James resist him?

How could he not kiss him?

He was still pressing Wade against the wall with a hand, but he moved to cup it around Wade's shoulder and pull him forward. Wade squeaked, but he was already in James's arms. James wrapped his arms around him, and when Wade opened his mouth, no doubt to say something stupid, James kissed him.

Wade's breath smelled of mint, probably because he'd brushed his teeth this morning. His lips were soft, and he yielded unexpectedly easily under James. James had presumed Wade would push back, but maybe he wanted to kiss James as much as James wanted to kiss him.

Which was something James hadn't predicted.

He hadn't expected Wade to want to kiss him or that he'd to want to kiss Wade. He didn't know where this had come from, but now that he'd started, he felt like he couldn't stop.

He pressed Wade harder against the wall. Wade grabbed his shoulders and tried to climb him like a tree, so it was good that the wall was there to support him. Wade managed to wrap his legs around James's waist, and James thrust forward. He wasn't hard yet, but it wouldn't be long before he was.

He had no idea what was happening or where this was going, but he needed Wade like he needed air. When had the little shit wormed his way under James's skin in a way no one else had been able to? What did it mean?

Nothing. It couldn't mean anything because of who they were. That didn't mean James was going to stop kissing Wade. If this was the only time they did this, he wanted to take full advantage of it.

He growled and lightly bit on Wade's lower lip. Wade whimpered and kissed him back harder, but James could feel the moment he fully realized what they were doing. He froze, his entire body going tense.

James quickly stepped away from the wall. Wade's legs slid to the ground, and James knew he needed to give him space. He didn't know what might happen if Wade felt crowded, but it wouldn't be good.

"What the fuck?" Wade muttered. He touched his lips, which were red and shiny.

For a second, James allowed himself to feel smug at the thought that he'd caused that. He'd reduced Wade to whispering *what the fuck* and seemed to have taken the ability to say anything else for a few seconds away from him.

Wade cleared his throat. "Look, the kiss was nice and everything, and I'm not going to say I didn't like it. I'd like you to kiss me again, and maybe for us to do more. But this is the wrong place to do it. Besides, you're an asshole. I can't do this with you when you're going to treat me like a child and when you don't believe one word that comes out of my mouth."

James stared. Everything Wade was saying made sense. Why would he want to kiss James when James had been obvious in his distaste for him? But Wade had willingly kissed James back. James felt they were in the same spot and that neither of them knew what to do.

"Besides, you don't even like me," Wade continued. "Why did you do that? Was it a way for you to shut me up? Or maybe to deal with the tension?"

"Who says I don't like you?" James asked. His voice was a little gravelly, and he could see the effect it had on Wade.

Wade's cheeks flushed, and he stared down at his feet. "I think that the way you've been talking to me and treating me points to the fact that you might hate me."

"I don't." And that was the truth. James didn't know how he felt about Wade, but it wasn't hate.

He didn't kiss people he hated.

Wade looked up at James. "Well, if you don't hate me, I don't think I'd want to be the person you do hate."

James didn't know what to say or how to explain himself. "We should go home," he whispered, hoping that what had happened between them would convince Wade to follow him.

That was the wrong thing to say. It distracted Wade from the kiss and reminded him why he was there.

He glared at James and straightened his back, and James knew he was in for a fight.

"Is that why you kissed me? Were you trying to distract me so you could convince me to come home with you? Or did you think I'd fall into your arms and allow you to decide for me? Because let me tell you, that kiss was nowhere near good enough to get me to do that."

"You're doing everything on your own, Wade. I never said or thought that."

But Wade wouldn't listen. "I don't care why you're here. I know why I am, and if you're not going to help me, then you need to stay out of my way. I'll find Mark dead or alive and give Dustin closure. I care about my friends, something you don't seem to understand, but I don't need you to understand. I just need you to leave me alone." He pushed James away and walked off.

James should go after him, and he almost did, but he could tell Wade wouldn't take that well. He didn't know what to do, but luckily, he wasn't an alpha. He didn't need to be the one to make decisions.

Chance would do that for him.

He took out his phone and followed Wade, keeping a reasonable distance. He could still see Wade, and while Wade probably knew he was behind him, he wouldn't feel boxed in.

Chance answered after a few rings. "Well? Have you convinced him to come home?"

"You should know better. When has anyone ever convinced Wade to do something he doesn't want?"

Chance chuckled. Now that he was sure Wade was safe, he sounded more relaxed about the situation.

James couldn't say the same. He needed to go home and protect the pack, and instead, he was here babysitting Wade.

And, apparently, kissing him.

"True," Chance said. "Well, you can't drag him back home, so maybe you could leave him there and come back. He's an adult, and while I don't like knowing he's putting himself in danger, there's nothing we can do to force him."

"I kissed him," James blurted out.

There was no answer, just shocked silence. James had shocked himself twice in a handful of minutes—first by kissing Wade, then by confessing it to Chance—so he understood.

But he wasn't talking to his alpha right now. He was talking to one of his best friends, and he hoped Chance would tell him what to do. Maybe he'd even convince James that it hadn't meant anything and that he'd just been trying to shut up Wade.

Chance laughed again. "I don't believe this. I was right."

James scowled, scaring a little old lady that had been walking past him. She scurried away, and he scowled harder—why was she even afraid of him? What did she expect he'd do, attack her in the middle of the street?

"You weren't. I don't like him." James was sure of that.

"The fact that you kissed him begs to differ. How was it? Did he kiss you back, or did he beat the shit out of you?"

James rubbed the back of his neck. "He kissed me back. I don't know why I kissed him, but it was a one-time thing."

Chance tsked. "Are you sure? Because it doesn't have to be.

If I was right and you've been bickering with Wade because you're trying to push him away, you need to get your head out of your ass. You're going to lose him otherwise."

James looked at Wade, who'd found a coffee shop and had slipped inside. He probably needed his morning caffeine dose and enough pastries to feed a small army. That was what James had seen him eat the few times they'd had breakfast as a family, so he knew Wade would be in there for a while, maybe even long enough for him to wrap his mind around what he'd done and decide why he'd done it.

Because it hadn't just been to shut Wade up.

CHAPTER FIVE

Wade sipped on his coffee, trying not to think about the man standing outside. James hadn't followed him inside the coffee shop, but Wade wasn't sure if it was because of the kiss or because he was on the phone. At the moment, he was pacing the sidewalk in front of the coffee shop, his attention on the call. It wasn't hard for Wade to guess it had to be Chance, and he wondered if the alpha was telling James to drag Wade back home. If James tried, he'd have a fight on his hands because Wade wasn't going willingly. He wasn't done here and wouldn't leave until he was.

He poked at his second pastry, trying to get his thoughts into order. Unfortunately for him, everything in his mind wanted to focus on James. He had so many questions about what happened that he wouldn't know where to start asking.

Why had James kissed him? Why had it felt like it was more than just a kiss? For a moment, Wade had been ready to let James fuck him against the wall. He'd been that far gone, and he didn't understand.

He'd had a crush on James before, but he'd told himself it was over because James was a jackass. That was still true, but then, what about the kiss? And what about James telling Wade he didn't hate him?

Nothing made sense. Wade wanted to push James until he got answers, but he wasn't here to moon over James, so he tried to move his attention in the right direction.

Taking his phone out, he ignored the dozens of texts he'd gotten and opened the notes app. He quickly wrote down everything he'd learned from Dustin's father. The attackers had never shifted, which probably meant they couldn't. Wilson had said they'd killed most of the clan members with knives—the thought made Wade shudder a little—and shifters wouldn't have done that. Wade would have been surprised if they hadn't used magic in some way, though. Even if a shifter couldn't shift, they wouldn't go down without a fight. The mages might have easily killed the weaker members of the clan, but what about the strong young men like Mark? It didn't make sense that only a handful of members had survived, which meant magic had been used, and not just to block them from shifting.

Wade tapped his fingertips on the table. He might be in trouble if the mages could so easily use magic. Even if he found Mark, how was he going to get him out of wherever he was being kept? The mages wouldn't let him go if they were using him for their magic.

Wade swallowed. The other alternative was that Mark was dead and Wade was putting himself in danger for no reason, but he wasn't ready to contemplate that. Mark had to be alive. Wade wouldn't stop trying to find him until he had him in front of him, so he needed to believe it.

His phone started vibrating in his hand, and he narrowed his eyes at Dustin's name on the screen. He was the only person he'd take a call from. Everyone else had gotten a group text, so they knew what was happening. Dustin probably wanted details, and since it was his brother that Wade was looking for, Wade couldn't very well not tell him anything.

"Hey, Dustin," he said.

"Why did I have to hear from Houston that you ran away?"

Wade spluttered. "I didn't run away. I'm not a surly teenager."

"You're not usually surly, but you do act like a kid sometimes. What were you thinking? What are you doing, Wade?"

Wade wasn't offended that Dustin didn't sound more enthusiastic. He was worried. "I'm going to find your brother. I told you I would."

"You did, but it's not your job."

"It doesn't matter."

There was a moment of silence. Dustin wouldn't yell at Wade. Wade didn't think he'd ever heard Dustin yell except the few times he'd fought with James, and that had been entirely James's fault. He was a dickhead to everyone, not just Wade.

"I do want my brother back, but it doesn't mean I want to lose you in the process," Dustin eventually said.

"You won't. I understand that I'm putting myself in danger, but I'm doing it willingly. Besides, I'm being careful. I promise."

Dustin sighed. "I won't try to convince you to come home because I know that nothing will get through to you when you're like this. Tell me what you found out."

Wade went through the conversation he'd had with Dustin's father. He told Dustin about the attackers wearing black masks and using knives, and while Dustin was silent as he listened, Wade was eager to get his thoughts on the situation. Dustin knew the clan better than anyone else Wade knew, so he could give precious insight into them and what the mages might have done.

"And that's it," he said when he reached the end of the story. "James got pissed and dragged me in the parking lot, then kissed me."

Wade snapped his mouth shut. He hadn't meant to say that last part, but it was too late. Hopefully, Dustin was focused on the rest of the story and hadn't heard the last bit.

But when had Wade ever been lucky?

"Hold on. You're telling me James kissed you?"

"Is there anything I can tell you to make you forget that

bit?"

"Definitely not."

"What do you mean James kissed him?" a voice asked.

Wade scowled. "You're with Houston." And now, Houston knew about the kiss, too.

"I am," Dustin confirmed. "We're in the car headed your way. We're almost there."

Wade blinked. "What? Why? You don't have to come." The area was full of bad memories for Dustin, and Wade didn't want him to have to deal with them.

"You're looking for my brother. I want to help, and I don't want you to do this on your own. So yes, we're coming. Now tell me about the kiss."

There was another burst of noise from Houston, and Wade wished he could reach through the phone and give him a good shake. Why did he have to listen in to this conversation?

But even if Wade had known Houston was listening in, he wouldn't have changed anything. He was freaking out about James and needed a friend to talk to. Maybe it would help distract Dustin from freaking out too much about his brother. "I don't know anything. It's not like we talked. After he was done kissing me, I kind of babbled that I liked it and that I wanted more, then told him to fuck off because he was an asshole and walked away."

Dustin laughed. "You have a knack for making every situation complicated."

"I'm not the person who made this complicated. James is. Why did he kiss me?"

"Probably because he's wanted to since the first time you opened your mouth in front of him."

"But he hates me."

"I don't know about that. I know the two of you have a complicated relationship, but coming from someone who tried to resist falling in love, pushing someone away doesn't mean you hate them."

"What do you think about this, then? Because I need to know."

"I'm not talking for him, so everything I'm saying might be wrong, but have you ever thought about the fact that he keeps snapping at you and pushing you away because you scare him?"

Wade looked up. James wasn't on his phone anymore but hadn't come in. He was watching the area, his body tense as if he expected trouble. He probably wasn't wrong. Trouble often followed Wade. "Why would he be afraid of me? I'm not going to attack him."

"Not physically, but from what Houston told me about him, he's a loner. He's been entirely focused on the pack and his job for most of his life. He's never had any meaningful relationships, probably because he thought they would distract him from what he considered important. He's avoided falling in love, but maybe he knows he can't avoid you, and that scares him. Maybe he likes you more than he's ever liked anyone, and he doesn't know how to deal with that. Sometimes we try pushing away the things we want because we don't know what to do and we're scared."

Dustin was talking from experience. He'd resisted dating Houston because he'd been afraid, but now they were together and happy. Wade couldn't imagine either of them with someone else, and it made him wonder.

Was Dustin right? Had James kissed Wade because he wanted him? More importantly, had he been lashing out every time they were together because he was afraid of what was growing between them?

James didn't dare go into the coffee shop. He could see Wade glaring at him from inside as if he'd done something wrong.

For once, he was innocent of whatever Wade was holding against him. He wasn't willing to get into a fight with Wade right now, so he stayed where he was and hoped Wade would get him coffee.

Fighting here when they could be attacked at any moment would be the worst idea ever. Besides, James didn't know what would happen if they started. He felt off-balance because of the kiss, and he had no idea how to deal with everything. He wasn't one for emotions. He disliked them because they were messy and made people do stupid things.

Like kissing a guy that he was supposed to dislike in the parking lot.

Life was easier without emotions, and keeping most people away helped. James had a loving family and Houston and Chance, but he'd seen heartbreak and broken relationships too often. It had been easier to avoid all of that, and he had.

Until Wade had crashed into his world.

Wade and his family were changing so many things, and James didn't know how to deal with that. He didn't know if he could, which was why he'd stayed away. He wasn't sure he could keep doing that, though. If anything, Wade would eventually demand an explanation for the kiss, and he wouldn't let go until he had what he wanted.

The problem was that James didn't have an explanation. He didn't know why he'd kissed Wade beyond the fact that he'd wanted to and that it felt like he'd die if he didn't. He wouldn't have forced Wade into anything, but Wade had kissed him back, and James wanted to do it again.

As long as it didn't earn him a kick to the balls.

He heard the coffee shop door open and turned to check who it was. Wade stepped out, two coffees in his hands. James was pretty sure one of them was for him, but he didn't dare ask. He wouldn't put it past Wade to sip on both alternatively while staring him in the eyes.

But Wade held out one of the coffees, and when James didn't take it right away, he tilted his chin at it. "It's black, just like your soul."

James huffed out a laugh. "You know how I take my coffee?" He accepted the cup and took a sip, sighing in pleasure at the warm bitterness.

"You're obviously one of those guys who take it black because you think it makes you look strong or something."

"That thing has more sugar than coffee in it," James said, pointing at Wade's drink.

"And it makes me the man I am." Wade cradled his coffee to his chest as if he expected James to try to take it from him. "Now, what's our next step?"

James cocked his head. "Why do you assume we're going to work together on this? The smartest thing would be to go home."

There went Wade's smile. James wanted to give him anything he wanted just to see it again, but he owed it to Wade to be honest. His job was to protect Wade, and the best way to do that would be for both of them to head home.

"I'm not going home," Wade said. "You can leave if you want, though. Dustin and Houston are on their way, so I won't be alone for long."

James had been taking another sip of coffee, and when Wade startled him, it almost went down the wrong pipe. "What do you mean Houston and Dustin are coming?" he asked between coughing and trying to breathe again.

"You heard me. They're coming. Dustin said they were almost here."

James resisted the urge to chuck his coffee at Wade's head. "Houston is the pack beta. I'm head of security. If we're both here, who's keeping the pack safe?"

Wade didn't seem worried. "Chance is the alpha, isn't he? I'm sure he can deal with all of it on his own for a few days."

"Pack security isn't something you can easily dump on someone else. I was fine when I thought Houston was there to keep an eye on everything. But now? There's no way we can stay."

Wade finished his coffee while glaring at James. "Like I said, no one is forcing you to stay. You can go back and protect the pack or do whatever you want. I'm not going anywhere, and if you try to force me, you'll have a fight on your hands. I might be small, but I'm scrappy. Even if I don't win, you'll be in a world of pain."

James didn't doubt that. Wade had to be strong to have survived on the streets, as did everyone in his family. James was trained and would win if they ever got in a fight, but he had no intention of hurting Wade.

He just wanted to strangle him a little.

He rubbed his face. He was running on too little sleep, and his stomach was empty except for the coffee. This wasn't going to end well if he didn't check himself. Yelling at Wade and fighting with him would be the worst way to go about this. James had to be smart, and at the moment, that meant going along with Wade.

"Let's go back to the motel," he eventually said. "We could both use more rest, and that way, it'll be easier for Houston and Dustin to find us."

Wade stared at James as if he expected him to bite. That made sense, since James would have normally snapped at him, and they might have ended up exchanging blows in front of the coffee shop. James wasn't an idiot, though, contrary to what Wade seemed to think. Back at home, it was safe for him to pester Wade. Even if Wade stormed off, he'd be fine.

The same couldn't be said of the situation they were in now.

Wade was silent as he followed James toward the motel.

James hoped they'd have a few hours to nap, but by the time they got there, Houston's truck was already parked in the parking lot. Houston was leaning against it, and he waved and grinned at James when he saw him.

All of James's anger turned to him. He couldn't yell at Wade, but he *could* yell at Houston.

He stomped toward his friend, telling himself that Houston was doing this for the man he loved. But *this* was why emotions were messy. Houston's priority should be the pack, not Dustin.

"What the fuck are you doing here?" James snapped when he reached Houston.

"Looks like someone got up on the wrong side of the bed," Houston said. "Or maybe Wade isn't a good kisser?"

James snarled. "You should be with the pack, protecting Chance. He's alone, and anything could happen if someone tries to attack the pack."

"Chance will be fine. The entire pack will be, and we'll be going home soon, anyway. Stop worrying, James. Dustin and I are here because Dustin wants to find his brother, and we thought you could use some help."

James raked a hand through his hair. "I could use some help keeping the pack safe."

"Yeah, well, we're here with Chance's blessing, and we're not going anywhere. He's the alpha, and he gave an order. Are you going to go against it?"

James glared at his friend. Houston had to know there was no way James would do that. Chance might be their friend, but first and foremost, he was their alpha. If he gave an order, they obeyed it.

Even James.

"Look, Chance knows how to defend himself and the pack," Houston said gently. "Everything has been quiet for a while, and he's worried that whoever attacked the clan might target us eventually. He wants to know what's happening, and the best way to do that is to have us here, so let's not fight and focus instead on what's important here, all right?"

James sucked in a breath. Houston was right, of course. They needed to find out what had happened so they could keep the pack safe. "Fine. I'll tell you what's been happening but don't get your hopes up. It's not much."

Houston's smile widened. "Are you sure? Because kissing Wade sure sounds like you have a lot going on."

James had to resist the urge to hit his friend. Houston was here to help, not to bother him.

The problem was that Houston didn't seem to know that.

Dustin hugged Wade so tightly that Wade briefly wondered if he was going to crack his ribs. It felt like it, but Wade needed it, so he held on, hugging Dustin back just as hard.

"You scared me to death," Dustin whispered as he leaned back. He looked at Wade as if trying to find out if he was hurt. "When Theo told me you'd left during the night, I was ready to come after you right away, especially when he told me James had come after you. I was worried."

Wade grinned. "You thought we'd kill each other."

"The thought did cross my mind. You have to admit you and James have been bickering and fighting more often than anyone I've ever met. Or is that over now that you've kissed and made up?"

Wade shook his head and stepped away. "We've kissed, but I don't think we made up. We've been ignoring the kiss." But Wade couldn't stop thinking about it. He didn't know if he ever could.

James was a strong man. He had to be, to protect the pack, and feeling all that strength made Wade yearn for more. They hadn't been in the right situation, but Wade had no doubt that if they had, he and James would have ended up in bed.

And he didn't know how that was possible.

James was an asshole. He was snarky and bitter, and he was always poking at Wade. Wade should be running away screaming and telling him to fuck off, but instead, he wanted nothing more than to run toward him and jump into his arms.

His crush was back in full force.

He rubbed his eyes. He had no idea how to deal with any of this, and it would be easier to focus on the other situation at hand. "James is hot, but he's also an asshole, and I don't know what's happening," he admitted.

"Well, maybe think about what I told you earlier." Dustin squeezed Wade's shoulder. "Although even if I'm correct, it's not right for him to treat you the way he has. Don't let him walk all over you."

Wade snorted. "As if I've ever allowed anyone to do that. Now, why don't we focus on what our next step will be?"

Dustin stared at Wade for a moment before nodding. "We can do that. I read your notes to Houston, and he admits something is odd."

"It's the *not shifting* thing. There's no way the attackers were shifters, because if they had been, that was how they would have attacked." Excitement built in Wade's chest. He knew he was right. He might have never met a mage, but they had to be behind this.

And Wade would prove that.

"Running away in the middle of the night, Wade? Really?" Houston asked when he and James joined Dustin and Wade.

Wade glared at him, but there was no heat behind it.

Houston was like another brother to Wade. He didn't know him well yet, but Dustin was in love with him, and that was enough for Wade to welcome the guy into his life.

"I had to do something. Dustin needs to know what happened to his brother," Wade explained.

"I know, and I'm just teasing. I have no idea what to think about your mage idea, but I don't have anything better, so we might as well focus on that. How do we go about finding mages when we don't even know they exist for sure?"

That was the problem. Wade had to find out where to start trying to find Mark. He was sure the mages had him, and they had to live around here, but he didn't have any other information. He certainly didn't have anything that would guide him and the others to the mages.

"What we need is information," he said, looking at the other three. They seemed to have decided he was in charge of this investigation for some reason.

He had every intention of doing a good job.

"If the mages live around here, someone is bound to have noticed something," he continued. "I imagine that while the clan members frequently visited the town, the humans who live here permanently probably had a better chance to see the mages. Who would have noticed if something was odd with the people coming and going from town?"

Dustin shrugged. "People at the diner."

Wade grimaced. "We're not going back there. Your father is probably still sitting at his table."

"He doesn't have anything else to do anymore, so probably," Dustin agreed.

They all knew having Dustin confront his father right now wouldn't be a good idea, so they'd have to start somewhere else.

"What about the grocery store?" Houston offered. "If the mages live around here, they have to eat somehow. I doubt they rely on the diner for all their meals, especially if there are enough of them to take on a dragon clan. That means they've had to shop for a large group of people, and someone at the store is bound to notice that. They'll notice not just who's a stranger, but also the amount of food they're buying. It has to stand out."

Wade beamed. "That's a great idea."

"It's a horrible idea," James grumbled, but he followed when Wade and the others moved toward the street.

Wade was relieved to see James wasn't going anywhere. He felt safer with him here, even though he was pretty sure that James had wanted to strangle him at least a few times. Wade knew No matter how James felt, he'd never hurt Wade, and he'd make sure Wade, Dustin, and Houston were safe.

Things had been bumpy since last night when Wade had arrived in town, but now that Dustin was here, too, things would be different.

It only took them five minutes in the grocery store before someone stopped in front of them, clearly there for Dustin. "What are you doing here?" the man asked.

He was tall and somewhat thick at the waist, in his late thirties. He didn't look angry, but rather, wary as if he didn't know why Dustin was here and he expected him to do something nefarious.

Dustin stared at him for a moment. "It's good to see that you're all right after what happened, Francis. What about your family?"

Francis grimaced. "Helena is gone. She sacrificed her life for Ashley and Benjamin."

"They're all right?"

"They lost their mother, but physically, they're fine."

Wade's heart broke a little at the pain in the man's voice. He didn't have to ask to know that Helena had been his wife and the mother of his children. He'd lost so much, but so had the other survivors. From what Wade knew, they were barely a clan anymore, and Dustin's father had clearly given up. They didn't know what that meant and what the few clan members who were still around would do, but they might be in danger if the mages were still in the area.

"Can you tell me what happened?" Dustin asked gently. "We're trying to find Mark and the people who hurt the clan."

"You're going to get yourself killed."

"Maybe so, but the clan doesn't need me. It never did."

Francis stared at Dustin for a moment. Wade expected him to brush Dustin off, so he was surprised when the man nodded instead.

"I can't tell you much. We were attacked during the night. There was an explosion, and everything was a mess. I left the house to go find your father and get orders, but I shouldn't have. I thought Helena and the kids would be safe at home. I could never have imagined how many people were attacking and that we wouldn't be able to shift." He rubbed the center of his chest. "We're still stuck. I don't care about me, but the kids can't shift, and they're terrified. This has been horrific enough for them. If you can do anything to help them, I'll tell you whatever you want to know."

"We're looking for a large group of people. Maybe someone noticed strangers buying a lot of food or something. Or maybe you can tell us more about the people who attacked that night."

Wade discreetly took out his phone, ready to take notes. He didn't want to rely solely on his memory, just in case.

No matter how small the detail, anything could be important to find the mages and Mark.

They spent the entire day in town, talking to people and getting all the details they could. By the time they were done, James was exhausted and wanted nothing more than a shower, food, and a bed. He didn't even care about what order he got them in, although going to bed needed to come last. He wouldn't wake up until tomorrow morning if he went to sleep.

"We don't have anything solid," Wade was saying as he stared down at his phone. "Many people have seen groups of strangers, but they don't know where they came from or where they are. I don't see how this can help us get anywhere."

"Talking to the people in town was your idea," James snapped. "What did you think they would tell you? The address and phone number of your mages?"

Wade glared. "There's no need to be all snarky. I thought we were past that."

They had been, mostly. James knew that fighting with Wade would only succeed in pushing Wade away, and when he'd been alone to protect him, he couldn't afford that. With Dustin and Houston there, though, James knew Wade was safe, and between that and how exhausted he was, he'd let his guard down.

Wade got under his skin like no one else ever had, and James didn't know how to deal with that. The kiss had been one way to do so, but it seemed so far away now. It had only happened this morning, but it felt almost like a dream.

It was a dream James wanted to repeat, but he didn't think that would be possible, considering the way Wade was glaring at him. That was fine with him, because he didn't want to kiss Wade. The only thing he wanted to do was drag him back home where James would know he was safe, and it was hard to resist the urge to do so. When Wade was around, James seemed to turn into a caveman, and it wasn't like him.

James might be gruff and snarky, but he wasn't an asshole to most people. His main goal was to protect the pack and its members, and he didn't care if he hurt anyone's feelings as he did so, but the situation with Wade was nothing like what he was used to. He didn't know how to deal with Wade. He didn't know what to do with him or how to be nice to him.

But he sure knew how to fight with him.

James liked that Wade stood up to him. Usually, when he snapped at someone, they either ignored him because they knew it was for the best, or they cowered. Most pack members tried to stay out of his way, and the few who didn't, like Houston and Chance, didn't hesitate to tell James he was being a dick.

Wade was the same. He wasn't afraid, and James liked that probably a little too much. He suspected it was one of the reasons he was so attracted to Wade. He couldn't imagine being in a relationship with someone who would be afraid of him, but clearly Wade wasn't.

"Why did you kiss me?" Wade asked softly.

James glanced back, but Dustin and Houston were in a world that belonged only to them. They were walking down the street, holding hands and talking to each other. It was odd to see Houston so taken with someone, but also good. He deserved to be happy, and that was what Dustin did for him. Even if James hated Dustin—and he didn't, contrary to what most people thought—he'd want him in Houston's life just because of how he made Houston smile.

"Because you can tell me if it was only to shut me up," Wade added.

He always talked a lot to fill silences, something James found both annoying and endearing.

What the fuck was happening to him?

"I mean, people always tell me I talk a lot," Wade continued. "And I do. I'm not trying to deny that. I know a lot of people dislike it, but I can't help it. When I'm nervous, I talk. Oh, and when I'm angry. Sometimes when I'm hungry, too. It helps distract me."

James was pretty sure Wade always talked a lot—in contrast to himself, who was mostly silent. That was the best way to observe the world and get answers. James doubted he'd ever change, but he didn't feel the need to. He also didn't want Wade to change.

They might be the opposite when it came to their personalities, but it didn't mean they couldn't fit together. The problem was that James didn't know how to fit with anyone or even if it was at all possible.

His other problem was that he didn't have an answer for Wade.

"I don't know," he admitted. "I didn't do it to shut you up, although I can't deny it was nice to have you silent for a bit. It just felt like the right thing to do."

Wade peered up at James. He looked wary, but his expression softened after a moment. "You really don't know, do you?"

"I wouldn't lie to you," James said in a slightly harsher voice. He hadn't meant to say it like that, but he didn't know where he stood with Wade. He never knew how to react to him, what to say, or what was going to come out of Wade's mouth. He loathed the sensation of being lost, and he suspected that was why he often lashed out. It was easier to make Wade angry than to try to understand him. It was certainly easier to make him angry than to allow him in, which James wasn't sure he could do.

James glanced behind them, but Houston and Dustin were still at a distance, lost in each other. That was why James wasn't surprised when Wade stopped walking, and he did, too. He expected Wade to have something to say.

But he didn't expect Wade to kiss him.

This time, it was Wade who took *him* by surprise. He wrapped his arms around James's neck and pushed himself up on his tiptoes. Their lips slanted together, and James was tempted to cradle Wade into his arms and never let him go.

That strong emotion was the one that made James push Wade away. He wasn't one who panicked easily, but right now, he had no idea what was happening, and his first instinct was to put up his shield and fight back, even though this wasn't a fight.

The hurt expression on Wade's face made James reach for him, but Wade shook his head and took a step away. "Sorry about that. It was a bad idea, and you don't have to tell me not to do it again. I won't."

"That's not what I was going to say," James tried, but Wade wouldn't hear it.

His eyes narrowed. "What were you going to say, then? That you like me, but only as a friend? That while you don't hate me, you'd never touch me with a ten-foot pole? I get it, all right? You don't like me, and that's fine. I just thought the kiss earlier changed something."

"I don't know. Maybe it was just a kiss." Or maybe it was so much more. James didn't know, and he was completely lost, which wasn't something he was comfortable with.

For a second, Wade's expression crumbled. Then he stood up straighter. "Maybe it *was* just a kiss."

He turned and started walking again. James moved to go after him, but a strong hand clasped his shoulder. When he turned to snarl at whoever was stopping him, he found Dustin and Houston standing behind him.

"Let me guess. You fucked up," Houston said.

James groaned and rubbed his face with both his hands. "I don't even know how."

"Well, you're going to have to find out soon if you don't want to lose him. He's not going to hang around forever, especially when you're an asshole to him. Couldn't you just let him kiss you? Would it have killed you?"

It wouldn't have killed James, but it didn't mean it hadn't been terrifying, and that wasn't something James knew how to deal with.

But maybe he should learn.

CHAPTER SIX

Wade couldn't sleep. He and the others had been in town for a few days, but they had nothing to show for it. They still didn't know where the mages were. They had no idea what had happened to Mark. Wade wasn't sure what their next step would be, but James was becoming antsy. He wanted to head home, and Wade understood why.

But that was the only thing he understood about James.

Maybe Wade wouldn't feel as restless as he did if he and James hadn't made a mess of things between them. They'd blurred the lines, and neither of them knew how to deal with that. What were they supposed to do about the kisses? James had pushed Wade away when Wade had kissed him, which probably meant that whatever had happened between them was already over before it could start. Wade wasn't surprised, but he was hurt and didn't know how to deal with that. He kept telling himself it was for the best and that James was an asshole, anyway, but that wasn't helping.

It was one of the reasons he was awake in the middle of the night, staring at the ceiling.

There was nothing he could do about the mages or Mark. He'd tried everything, from talking to as many people as possible to going back to Dustin's father and even going to clan territory. That had been hard, and Wade hoped he'd never have to go back again. There hadn't been any bodies, they'd seen destroyed homes and suspicious dark spots on the ground that looked like blood. The air was heavy, and just thinking about how many people had died there had made

Wade's skin prickle. He could only imagine how hard it had been for Dustin.

Being in clan territory hadn't helped. They still didn't know where the mages were, and they were running out of time. If Mark was still alive, they wouldn't keep him that way for much longer, or at least Wade didn't think so. Mark could be trouble, and Wade was surprised the mages had selected him.

Grabbing any other dragon would have been much easier, so why go for the alpha's son? The mages were lucky that Wilson had decided not to go after his heir, but they couldn't have known that would happen. Maybe they hadn't realized who Mark was. Either way, they'd had Mark for too long, and Wade didn't like it.

With a huff, he pushed away the mattress and sat up. Staying in bed wasn't helping. If anything, it made him more nervous because not moving made him feel like he had ants under his skin. He might not be able to come up with a solution to his problems, but maybe taking a walk would help. It would make him sleepy at the very least, which was better than nothing. James would kick Wade's ass if he found out, but he wouldn't have the opportunity to. Wade wasn't planning on waking him up to let him know, although he'd leave a note to Dustin, just in case.

They'd come up with that tactic when they still lived on the streets, and it had kept them safe. Wade didn't anticipate getting in trouble tonight, but he'd rather be safe than sorry.

He quickly dressed, then opened the door of his room. Once outside, he paused and listened, but he couldn't hear anything that would indicate James had heard him. James was in the next room, and Wade half expected him to come out and berate him, but nothing happened.

Wade supposed that even James had to sleep sometimes. He was always tense and ready to act, and it had to be exhausting. Sometimes Wade thought James was overprotective, but he would never dare say that out loud. James would kick his ass.

Wade left the motel behind, but he wasn't sure where to go. He didn't want to go too far because he had every intention of going back to sleep eventually, but he also didn't want to stay too close in case James realized what was happening. Wade didn't want to fight with him right now, but he had no doubt that was what would happen if James got to him.

Why were they always bickering? It wasn't hate, at least not on Wade's side. No, he liked James, even knowing that he was an asshole most of the time. Wade had started to realize that it was a way for James to push people away. Who would want to get close to him when they couldn't stand him? But James wasn't a bad person. He might be gruff and unpleasant, but he cared for the pack, and the fact that both he and Houston were here made him anxious. He was afraid something would happen to the pack, and if it did, he'd feel guilty for the rest of his life because he hadn't been there.

They needed to find something or go home. Wade didn't want to go, but he couldn't deny that the four of them weren't making any progress and couldn't stay here forever. He hadn't made any promises to Dustin, but leaving without Mark would feel like a failure. Could they afford to stay for much longer, though?

Wade rubbed his forehead. He didn't have any answers, and he hated that.

The sound of quick footsteps behind him made him turn. He didn't have the time to see who was coming after him. Something hit him on the back of the head, and he cried out in pain. He tried to push the person away, but they were already pulling something over his head, probably so he couldn't see them.

"I don't have anything on me," he said with a cough. "But

I have money in my motel room. You just need to let me go there."

A hand grabbed his arm and pulled. It hurt, and he winced, but he did his best not to show how frightened and in pain he was.

"We don't need your money," a gruff voice said.

Wade realized why seconds later when they pushed him into what had to be a van. He tried to fight it, certain that if he went in there, he would never come back, but it was useless. Another pair of hands grabbed him, pulling him from the inside, and the only thing he could do was yield.

Dammit. He was being kidnapped.

At least he'd been smart about leaving his room in the middle of the night. These people probably didn't realize that he'd left a note and that eventually, someone would wake up and find it. Wade was glad he still had that habit.

It might just save his life.

There was no way to know if his note would be found in time, but he could only hope, and he did. Dustin would do everything he could to find Wade, and he wasn't the only one.

Wade wouldn't want to be these people once James got his hands on them.

He continued resisting, but it was useless. Something sparked against his back, and while he was in a world of pain and trying to keep his shit together, they pushed him again. He tumbled into what felt like the back of the van, and by the time he managed to scramble into an upright position, the door had been closed, and the van was moving.

Wade licked his lips. He still couldn't see anything, but he didn't need to. He knew who these people were.

"You're mages," he said.

Only silence met him. These people didn't want to answer, which would make sense. Not only were they used to keeping what they were a secret, but they probably despised shifters.

And Wade was a shifter.

But he had to try. He had to make them see that he didn't have anything to do with the clan. Maybe they'd targeted the dragons for a specific reason. If that was so, it would be best for Wade to explain that he wasn't a dragon.

"I don't want any trouble," he said. "I'm just here to find a friend's brother. I have no idea what happened, and I don't care. Just don't hurt me, all right?" His voice trembled slightly.

He was terrified. He'd thought he was safe after he and the others had moved to Mayport, and he would have been if he hadn't been an idiot. He didn't regret coming after Mark, but he did regret going for a walk on his own in the middle of the night.

But it was too late for regrets. The mages had him, and he was pretty sure that if they had their way, he wouldn't be alive for long.

The sound of someone pounding on the door made James jerk out of bed. It took him a second to remember where he was and what was happening, and by the time he did, he was crouching in a defensive position, ready to take on whoever was trying to come in.

But they weren't trying to come in. They were just knocking, albeit quickly and powerfully.

Something had happened.

James strode to the door and flung it open. Dustin stood on the other side, his eyes wide and his fist raised. He looked James up and down, his cheeks flushed, but he didn't look away.

James had on only his boxer briefs. He didn't like to feel constricted when he slept. "What's going on?" he asked. "It's the middle of the night." It was getting close to five AM, but they still could have slept for a few more hours. They spent their days talking to people and poking around town, and it wasn't like they had to get up early to do that. Talking to so many people was exhausting, and James needed time alone to recharge, dammit.

"Wade is gone."

Wade was gone? That wasn't possible. James blinked, sure he'd heard wrong, but Dustin was still staring. "What do you mean?"

"I woke up early, went to the bathroom, and saw there was a note under the door. Wade left it like we used to when we lived on the streets and one of us had to go off on their own. He said he went out because he couldn't sleep and that he'd be right back."

"Then I don't see what the problem is."

"He left me the note at two AM."

That wasn't good. "How do you know?"

James went back into the room, leaving the door open. Dustin stepped in, but James didn't give him much attention as he dressed.

"We always dated the notes and wrote the time we left them at. That way, we knew when someone was supposed to be home."

"So he's been gone three hours?"

"Something like that, yes. I went to his room, but it doesn't look like anything happened there. He just vanished."

But people didn't vanish. That meant something had happened to Wade, and as soon as James got his hands on him, he'd strangle him. Then he'd make sure Wade never went anywhere on his own ever again. Hadn't he learned his lesson?

James dressed in a matter of minutes, then followed Dustin outside. He wasn't surprised to see that Houston was up, too. The three of them stared at each other, and James knew he had to take the lead. Dustin was distraught, and Houston focused more on him than on finding Wade.

"Can I see the note?" James asked.

Dustin took a folded piece of paper out of his pocket and handed it over. It was nothing more than what Dustin had said. Wade just explained he was going for a walk at two AM earlier this morning and that he'd be right back.

Except he wasn't back.

"We need to call Chance," James said as he looked up. "He has to know one of his pack members is missing."

"Maybe Wade just isn't back yet," Houston offered.

James scowled at him. "He wouldn't do that. He'd know how worried Dustin would be, especially considering the circumstances."

Houston grimaced. "Right. Yeah, we need to call Chance."

But that wasn't enough. James needed to do more to find Wade, but how? They had no idea where he went or what had happened. Considering the circumstances, it was a good bet that he'd been kidnapped, but they still didn't know where to find them.

James pushed away the fear that was building in his chest. He was terrified that he was losing Wade before having the opportunity to tell him he cared about him. They hadn't talked much over the past few days, and it was entirely James's fault. Instead of opening up to Wade when Wade had tried kissing him, he'd pushed him away, and that could be the last thing he'd remember of Wade and that Wade would remember of him.

He was used to being an asshole, but he didn't like it right now.

But that just meant he had to find Wade. That way, they could make new memories, and James wouldn't have to worry about how Wade would remember him. Besides, Wade would be fine.

He had to be.

"I'm calling Chance," Houston said as he took out his phone.

James nodded and turned his attention to Dustin. "Come on. Let's walk around and see if we can find anything."

James didn't know where Wade would go, especially in the middle of the night. They'd explored most of the town but hadn't found any clues about any mages or Mark's location. It meant Wade could be anywhere. What if he'd noticed something strange and had decided to investigate on his own? James tried to remember where they'd been yesterday. They'd visited the diner again, even though Dustin hadn't wanted to see his father. From there, they'd gone back to the grocery store.

They started at the diner. It was already open but empty of people except for the waitress and the cook. They were quietly talking, and when James poked his head in to ask if they'd seen Wade, they both shook their heads.

Dustin was wringing his hands as they walked, while Houston was talking to Chance. James wanted to tell Dustin that this wasn't his fault and that even if something had happened to Wade, Dustin had nothing to do with it, but he wasn't sure it would be welcome. He wasn't the best person to comfort people, especially people who were panicked. The only thing that would make Dustin feel better would be to see Wade, which meant James had to find him.

"I don't think he would have gone too far from the motel," he said as they retraced their steps back there. "I know I wouldn't if I went for a walk in the middle of the night. I'd want to be close by so that if I get sleepy, I can get back to bed right away."

Dustin nodded. "I think you're right about that."

The problem was that there were too many places where someone could have hidden and grabbed Wade while he walked past. James kept his eyes open as the three of them walked, but there was nothing. It was as if the earth had opened up and swallowed Wade, and James tightened his hands into fists at the thought.

He wanted to hit something, or even better, someone. He wanted to make the people who'd taken Wade pay. He couldn't even imagine what Wade was going through right now, and it scared him that he was so afraid.

"What do you mean, a tracker?" Houston suddenly asked.

James froze and turned to his best friend. What was he talking about? Who had a tracker?

Houston raised a finger. "Wait. I'm putting you on speaker, because James and Dustin need to hear this, too."

He glared at Houston a little, which seemed to confuse him because he blinked and cocked his head in question. James didn't care.

He focused on the call, and as soon as he heard Chance's voice, he asked, "Who has a tracker?"

"Wade and every member of Theo's family. Even you, Dustin, remember?"

Dustin's cheeks flushed. "I forgot," he whispered.

James glared at him, too, but he didn't stay focused on him for too long. "So you know where Wade is?"

"Theo is opening the app right now. We'll send you the coordinates as soon as we have them, but I don't know if going in there on your own is a good idea. We don't know what these people are capable of. They took on a dragon clan, which means it can't be good. You can't risk going in there on your own."

"They could be hurting him." And the panic that seized James's chest at the thought was enough to make him breathless.

"I know, but I already sent people out. It'll take them several hours to reach you, but I need you to stay put in the meantime."

James didn't know if he could do that. For the first time ever, he was thinking about disobeying a direct order. He didn't know how it made him feel, but if this was needed to keep Wade safe, he'd do it.

Because he cared about Wade. Because he was falling in love with him. Because Wade was more important than the only thing that had been important to James before meeting him.

Wade wasn't sure what had happened when he woke up. He remembered going on a walk and being kidnapped, but how had he become unconscious? *That* was what he didn't remember, and for a moment, he blinked at the ceiling.

This was how he'd ended up in trouble. Was it so bad to stare at the ceiling for a few hours? No, it wasn't, even though clearly, Wade had thought so earlier. He'd give anything to go back to the motel and stare at its ceiling, but he doubted he'd be let go.

He tried to move, but he couldn't. He wasn't at all surprised to realize he was tied up, and while he didn't like it, at least whatever had been covering his face was gone. That meant he could see around himself, and he took advantage of that. He needed every detail he could find about where he was.

The place he was in looked like a cross between a bedroom and a prison cell. He was stretched out on a metal frame bed, his hands tied together in front of him. His ankles were tied, too, and for a second, he imagined himself trying to run away while hopping down a hallway. He almost chuckled, but he was in trouble and couldn't afford to be distracted.

James was *so* going to kick his ass once he found him.

Wade had no doubt James would. As soon as he realized something was happening, he would come running. Wade had left a note with Dustin, but that wasn't the only thing. After he and his family had settled down in Mayport, they'd all agreed they wanted to get trackers. They were afraid something would happen to one of them and the others wouldn't know, and while Wade suspected it was because of what they'd gone through in the past and that it wasn't necessary, he'd gone along with it. It helped soothe him to know where his family was just by opening an app on his phone, and while he hadn't thought it would come in handy during a kidnapping, he'd have to remember to kiss Theo as soon as he was home, because his old alpha was the one who had the idea and to arranged for the trackers.

It was easy to forget about the tracker, because Wade couldn't feel it. Besides, they'd all been busy setting up their new lives, and Wade had only used the app a few times to keep an eye on the rest of his family.

Dustin was in town, and he had his cell phone. That meant he knew where to find Wade and that Wade just had to wait until they got to him. As long as the mages didn't hurt him, he'd be fine.

There wasn't much to the room. There was a window, but the curtains were drawn, so Wade couldn't see anything. A little light was coming in from under the curtain, which meant it was morning already. That meant that if Dustin hadn't found the note yet, he would soon.

Wade just had to wait.

The sound of footsteps coming closer made him tense. He briefly wondered what he was supposed to do. Act as if he was still unconscious? That was probably for the best, so he closed his eyes just in time to hear the door open.

It squeaked a little. Then nothing happened for a few seconds. Wade could feel someone staring at him, and it made him want to squirm in the worst way. Instead, he kept his breathing calm and steady. He had no idea who this person was and what they wanted, and he didn't want to find out. He just wanted to get out of there.

The person at the door walked into the room and closed the door behind them. There was the sound of something landing on a hard surface, and it was hard not to peek.

"I know you're awake," a male voice whispered.

Wade considered not moving, but he was too curious. He opened his eyes, quickly glancing around to find the person who'd spoken.

A young man was standing by the dresser. Wade could see a tray on it, and his stomach growled. He hoped this guy had brought him food, but he wasn't about to ask. It wasn't like he'd starve, anyway. James and the others would be here soon, and once they were done kicking mage asses, they'd take Wade out for breakfast.

Or at least, that was what Wade was trying to convince himself of.

He and the man stared at each other for a moment. The man couldn't be much older than Wade, if even that, probably early twenties if Wade had to guess. His skin was pale, as if he didn't see the sun often enough, and it was peppered with freckles. The man's auburn hair flopped around his face, and he pushed a strand back behind his ear.

Wade almost gasped at the sight of the scar that ran from the man's right eye down to his mouth. It didn't take away from the man's beauty, but it made Wade want to find the person who'd done that to him and hurt them. It couldn't have been one of the dragons. It was a scar, not a fresh wound, which meant it had been there for a long time.

"Are you going to stare at me all day?" Wade asked eventually. He probably shouldn't be snarky with one of the people who'd kidnapped him, but he couldn't help it.

The man jumped and looked guilty, which wasn't something Wade had expected. He grabbed the tray, then put it down and came closer to Wade instead.

"I brought you some food, but I need to untie you so you can eat." He hesitated. "Are you going to attack me if I do?"

"No. I'm not going to be able to run away from this place. You're the only one in here, but I'm ready to bet there are all sorts of guards and security stuff around to make sure no one can leave."

The man hesitated, then nodded. "There are."

Wade held out his hands. The man hesitated for a second longer, but eventually, he came closer and untied Wade's hands.

Wade rubbed them to get the feeling back into his fingers. The man was already working on untying Wade's ankles, and while Wade wanted to point out he didn't need his feet to eat, he didn't dare.

"Thank you," he whispered once he was free.

The man nodded. "I'm Lester."

Wade cocked his head. Why was Lester telling him his name? "I'm Wade." Lester seemed fearful, but Wade didn't know why. Was it because he was afraid someone would hurt him for untying Wade? Was there something else there that Wade couldn't see?

He didn't know how many mages belonged to this group, but there was bound to be at least one who disagreed with what they'd done, right? And what if that someone was Lester?

Wade couldn't afford to let this opportunity slip through his fingers.

"I need your help," Lester said as he leaned closer. His tone became a whisper, and Wade stayed still as he listened. "They're hurting him, and they're going to kill him if someone doesn't take him away," Lester said in a rush. "I tried to free him, but it didn't work. I need help."

He had to be talking about Mark. "And you think I can help

you? Because I'm a prisoner, too," Wade pointed out.

Lester swallowed and looked around as if he expected someone to be there, spying on him. "I can help. I'll get you and the dragon shifter out. But I can't do it on my own."

Wade slowly nodded. "All right. How do we do this?"

Lester blinked. "You're going to help?"

"I'm pretty sure it's my only possibility of making it out of this place, so yes. I just have a question."

"What?"

"What about you? What's going to happen to you when someone finds out you had something to do with the escape?"

Lester grimaced. "It won't be pretty. I'm used to it, so you don't have to worry about me."

He raised his hand to his face but stopped before touching the scar. Wade knew that was what he'd been about to do, though. This man was a mage, as were the people he lived with, but there was clearly no love between them. Wade needed answers and wouldn't get them once he and Mark left.

If they even managed to do that in one piece.

But maybe there was a way for him and the pack to find out more about the mages. "Come with us," he said, reaching for Lester.

Lester took a step back. "What?"

"Come with us. I don't want to leave you here if they're going to hurt you. I know you don't trust me, but I promise we won't hurt you or make you a prisoner."

Lester didn't have a reason to trust Wade, but Wade hoped he would.

James stared at the house. He probably wouldn't have noticed it if he hadn't known Wade was in there somewhere. It was well hidden between the trees, deep in the forest, and he wasn't surprised the dragons had never realized it was there. It wasn't massive, but it would easily house a dozen people, maybe more if they didn't mind sharing their living spaces and not having privacy.

It looked abandoned, but James was pretty sure that was because of a spell or whatever the mages did. If he cocked his head in a certain way, he could see through it, so he knew that the house was well-kept. This had to be a security system. If people thought the place was abandoned, they wouldn't nose around and they wouldn't find the mages.

They'd found the mages, just like Wade had known they would.

He would be so incredibly smug once they got him out that James briefly considered leaving him here. He was afraid something would happen to him, though. Besides, he needed to tell him he wanted him.

James was done resisting. It was useless. He and Wade liked each other. They'd yelled, screamed, and fought. Yet they'd still ended up kissing, and James had fallen in love with Wade. There was no escaping that, and maybe it was time for James to stop running. He hated that it had taken Wade being kidnapped for him to realize that, and he had no doubt he'd have to grovel, but he was ready to do just that.

As long as he got Wade back in one piece.

"How do we do this?" Dustin whispered.

He was pale but looked strong, and James knew he wouldn't hesitate to do whatever he had to in order to save his friend.

James and Dustin looked at each other. "I'm not sure," James admitted. "We don't know anything about these mages. What kind of security system they have, or anything like that. I don't know if going inside is smart, but I don't know how else we could get to Wade."

Dustin trusted him and Houston to know what to do. He

hoped he wouldn't break that trust by not being able to save Wade.

"We need to find out what's going to happen if we go in," he whispered.

"How?"

James opened his mouth to tell Dustin he had no idea when the sound of a door creaking open made him stop. He peered at the back door of the house. It had opened just a little, and as he watched, it opened fully. Two figures slipped out, one of them supporting the other. A third person came out behind them and closed the door, but this one paused instead of running away from the house like the first two figures had.

"Lester," someone hissed.

James would have recognized that voice anywhere.

It looked like he shouldn't have worried. He'd wanted to save Wade, but Wade was saving himself. He was going to be so smug about that, too, dammit.

"I don't know if I can do this," the third person said. That had to be Lester, though James had no idea who Lester was.

"What are they going to do to you if they find out you helped us escape?" Wade asked.

Lester reached for his face. James was too far away to be able to see him well. It was the middle of the day, but the house and the three men close to it looked somewhat hazy. That was why he hadn't been sure Wade was one of them when they'd snuck out, and he still didn't know who the third figure was. He hoped it was Mark for everyone's sake, but it was impossible to be sure of that.

"They'll hurt me," Lester whispered.

There was a world of pain in his voice, as if he'd already been through this more than once. He probably had. It sounded as if even though he was a mage and part of this group, the others wouldn't hesitate to hurt him. James didn't think Lester was lying, because there was no way to fake that kind of pain.

James almost groaned. Wade was going to want to adopt him, wasn't he?

"Come with us," Wade said. "I told you I would protect you, and I meant that. Come on. We have to get to the nearest road before they realize we're gone."

James and Dustin looked at each other. Dustin was already smiling, and James suspected that the only reason he hadn't rushed forward was that Houston was clinging to his hand. James raised one of his, getting both of their attention. He gestured at himself, then at the trio, who was still bickering over whether or not Lester should leave.

"I'll go. Stay here."

Dustin shook his head. "We should all wait here. What if there's some spell that would alert the mages that someone is close to the house?"

That was a good question. James would rather stay where he was, but his instincts were telling him he needed to get to Wade. The best way to have Wade back without moving would be to call out to him, and while James was hesitant because someone might hear, the trio was making enough noise that someone probably would, anyway.

"Wade," he whispered as loudly as he dared.

Wade froze, then frantically looked around. "James?" he called out.

He needed to be more discreet, dammit. "We're here. The three of you need to hurry."

"I'm staying," Lester said, frantically looking around as if he expected James to jump out of a bush.

Wade obviously couldn't let that happen. James had expected it, so he wasn't surprised when Wade shuffled back toward Lester, dragging the third man along with him. He grabbed Lester's hand and pulled, and even though it couldn't be easy for him to drag two people, he managed.

"Shut up and come with us," he told Lester. "We'll protect you. That's my boyfriend, and he'll make sure nothing happens to you, all right?"

Houston arched a brow at James and mouthed the word *boyfriend,* but James flipped him the bird and waited. He didn't care what Wade called him. He had every intention of becoming Wade's boyfriend soon—if he wasn't already.

The three of them watched the trio come closer. James rushed forward as soon as they were just a few feet away. Houston and Dustin followed, going straight for the third person, who had to be Mark. Dustin cried out when he saw the state his brother was in, but they didn't have time.

"Come here," James gruffly said as he grabbed Wade's shoulder. He pulled him into his arms and wrapped himself around him, burying his nose against the top of Wade's head and inhaling his scent.

Wade was fine. Everyone was.

Well, except Mark and possibly the rest of them if they didn't get out of here quickly.

"We have to go," Lester whispered. "They're going to realize something's happened soon."

Wade nodded. "Come on." He turned to James. "Please tell me you didn't come on foot."

"We didn't. The car is parked close by, so let's go."

Dustin and Houston grabbed Mark and hauled him up. Together, it was easier to drag him away, with Wade taking Lester's hand and pulling him forward. From up close, James could see what Lester had been touching when he reached for his face. It would have been impossible not to see the scar. Clearly, these mages didn't just attack dragon shifters. They also attacked each other, which meant they were dangerous and ruthless.

James was glad he'd gotten Wade out, or rather, that Wade had gotten himself out. He'd been ready to burst in and beat up anyone he saw, but there had been no way to know how the mages would react. James didn't want to risk not being able to shift. He could think of nothing worse except losing Wade or one of his friends.

But everyone was all right. There was no way to know what state Mark was in, but they'd find out soon. In the meantime, they were together, and everyone was safe.

Wade squeezed James's hand. "I knew you'd come for me."

James could only nod. "Always. Whatever trouble you get yourself into, I'll always come for you. I swear."

The smile Wade gave him told James that the words he couldn't say had been heard, anyway. Wade knew how he felt. No matter what happened, James would never let anyone or anything hurt him. They might have a lot to talk about and figure out between them, and they would.

James wouldn't have it any other way.

Chapter Seven

Wade threw his head back as James made his way up his body. James was heavy on top of Wade, but Wade didn't care. He almost hadn't gotten this, and it would have been James's fault.

Sometimes Wade still wanted to slap sense into his boyfriend.

But not while James was driving him wild with pleasure.

He nibbled on Wade's neck as Wade dug his fingers into his shoulders and arched his back. He needed to be closer, but that wasn't possible unless James got to the point and finally fucked him.

But James had already learned how to deal with Wade. Their fights didn't get as bad as before, but they still bickered regularly. Wade felt it wouldn't be them if they didn't, and he didn't mind. Everything was good as long as they weren't nasty to each other.

It really was. Wade couldn't have imagined having this kind of relationship with James when James had been so bitter with him before, but somehow, it worked, and Wade had never been so happy.

He jolted when James suddenly bit on the skin where Wade's neck met his shoulder. He scowled and pushed James away, but he was smiling, and Wade couldn't stay angry at him for long anymore.

"That hurt, asshole," he complained.

James's hand found Wade's cock. "Yeah?"

Wade sucked in a breath. "That doesn't, though."

"No?"

James ran his fingertips up and down Wade's cock before wrapping them around it. He tugged, and Wade clung to him harder. He never wanted this to end. He almost hadn't gotten it, and sometimes, he still woke up after a nightmare in which he never left the coven. It had been close, but he was safe and in James's arms.

And he was never leaving them.

James sucked in the skin he'd bitten. He played with Wade's body in a way no one ever had, as if he already knew exactly how to drive Wade to the brink. Maybe he did, even though they hadn't been together long. He'd always been good at driving Wade nuts, after all.

Wade moved his hands to James's arms and pulled him up so they could kiss. Their bodies pressed together, and Wade wrapped his legs around James's waist. He never wanted to let go. Being the target of James's anger had been thrilling, but being the target of his love was everything.

They moved together, linked as one. No matter how things had been between them before, James touched Wade like he was precious now. He made Wade feel special and even loved, and Wade basked in that as he hung on tight and came. He shuddered through the pleasure, hanging on for dear life until James slumped on top of him.

For a moment, Wade let everything sink in. He was safe. He was happy. He had a family and a home, and while he'd almost lost all of that, he hadn't.

When he started having trouble breathing, he pushed James away. "You're heavy."

James rolled off, but he didn't go far. He settled on his side and hooked an arm around Wade's waist, holding him close as if he wasn't ready to let him go.

"You weren't complaining five minutes ago," he teased.

"Five minutes ago, you didn't feel heavy."

James kissed Wade's temple. "Sorry."

Wade almost couldn't believe that James was apologizing. "Don't do that."

"Do what?"

"Apologize for something so minor. I'm fine. You didn't hurt me or anything, and there's nothing to apologize for."

James tensed, then relaxed. "I'm so scared I'm going to fuck this up that I feel the need to apologize for everything." He pressed his forehead against Wade's shoulder. "I don't know what I'm doing, Wade. I want to give you everything you deserve, but I don't know if I can. I have no idea how to do it."

At least he was admitting it, which wasn't something Wade had expected. It was a step forward, which was more than Wade could have hoped for.

It would have been easier for James to stay away. He wouldn't have to learn how to be in a relationship, and Wade would be the first to admit that often he wasn't easy to be with. He'd had to harden up when he'd lived on the streets, and most days, he was a bit feral. Their personalities were strong and clashed against each other, which complicated things even more.

But they could do this. Wade had faith in them.

"You don't need to know what you're doing," he said, running a hand up and down James's arm. "We'll figure it out together. It's not like I've had many relationships, and while it's true that we were messed up in the beginning, I think that as long as we talk things out instead of yelling at each other, we'll make it."

James looked up. "Yeah? Sometimes, I wonder why you put up with me. You're a gorgeous man with an even more gorgeous personality. Anyone would be happy to have you, yet you settled on a grumpy fuck like me."

Wade kissed him because he could and because he wanted to. "You're *my* grumpy fuck, James. You might be a stick in the mud, but you're mine, and that's all that matters to me. We can make this work."

"I never want to hurt you."

Wade didn't say he already had, but they both knew it was true. Wade had hurt James, too, but that was in the past, and they needed to move on. "Then don't. I'm sure you'll fuck up sometimes, and so will I, but I'll always tell you when you're a dick, and I know you'll do the same for me. It can be us against the world, but we'll have to work for it."

"I'm not afraid of hard work, and I always knew you'd be hard work."

Wade stuck out his tongue. "Yeah, well, I might have chosen you, but you chose me, too."

"And that's never going to change."

Wade wouldn't have wanted any other answer. He snuggled closer, knowing that James would have to get up soon to deal with everything. They'd only been back one day, and while they'd found Mark, the problems were only starting. The coven would be gunning for the pack for what Wade had done, and it was a scary thought.

James sighed. "I wish I could stay in bed with you."

"But you have to go to work."

"Yeah. I need to talk to Mark and Lester." James scowled. "I don't trust either of them, but especially not Lester."

"That's because you're an asshole who doesn't trust anyone."

"I trust you."

And that was a balm on Wade's heart. Knowing that he was one of the few people in the world that James trusted made everything he'd gone through worth it. "And I love that, but I can't be the only person you trust. You need to open your heart."

"It's open enough," James grumbled.

Wade shouldn't find it adorable, but he did. Maybe James's

heart *was* open enough. He had his family, Chance, Houston, and now Wade. It was enough for him, but Wade wasn't like him. He wanted more people in his life, and he wanted to help Lester.

He couldn't say he trusted Lester, but he didn't think Lester was a bad person. It wasn't his fault he'd grown up in a coven bent on killing every shifter they could get their hands on. He could have gone along with it, but instead, he'd helped Wade and Mark escape, and now, he was stuck with the pack. He had to live with a bunch of people who thought he'd kill them if they turned their backs for only a second, and that couldn't be easy.

"You don't have to trust Lester, but maybe give him a chance," he told James. "He could have looked the other way. He could have stayed with the coven and ignored Mark and me, because it would have been so much easier for him. Instead, he lost everything to do the right thing. He deserves to be allowed to show everyone that he's not a danger, and he deserves a fresh start."

"I still don't like him."

Wade grinned and looked down at James. "Remember when I said I'd tell you if you were being an asshole? Well, you are."

James huffed, but he didn't sound or look angry. "Fine. I'll talk to him and Houston and Chance. We'll see what they say. I don't know what will come out of it. But you know Chance. He has a soft heart, and it didn't get any better after he met Theo."

"Depends on your definition of better."

James stared at Wade for a moment before nodding. "I suppose you're right. My life certainly got better since he allowed you and your family to stay with the pack, so maybe I should give him the benefit of the doubt."

"You should. You gave it to me, after all."

"And I haven't regretted it."

He never would. Wade would make sure of that.

About the Author

Catherine is the creator of several series, most of them paranormal, including the Whitedell Pride Series and the Gillham Pack Series. While she graduated in translation, she decided to go the writer's way because it was more fun to create her own stories and characters.

She's been living in Italy for more than twenty years, but she's a daughter of the North—Belgium to be precise—and she misses it so much that she's already planning to move back.

She loves pizza—probably too much—her son, her pets, and of course, books. She sneaks some reading time into her schedule every time she has five minutes free from writing, demands from her various pets and son, and lastly, housework.

Connect with her:

lievens.catherine@gmail.com
BookBub: https://www.bookbub.com/authors/catherine-lievens
Website: https://authorcatherinelievens.com/
Facebook: https://www.facebook.com/catherine.lievens.9
Facebook Group: https://www.facebook.com/groups/411788002341528/
Twitter: https://twitter.com/authorCLievens
Newsletter: http://eepurl.com/c-uvKn

www.ingramcontent.com/pod-product-compliance
Lightning Source LLC
LaVergne TN
LVHW020643100826
845148LV00012B/2317
* 9 7 8 1 4 8 7 4 3 9 6 0 6 *